# REACH FOR THE SKY

GWEN KNIGHT

*gwen* ♡
RT2018

REACH FOR THE SKY

*Dear Reader,*

I have to say this book was my biggest challenge yet. I am forever attracted to the "Knight in Shining Armor" sort. So when I was invited to participate in the Bad Boy Alpha project, I was intrigued! I'd never written the bad boy as the main character, but I had so much fun with Wyatt. I hope you love him as I have come to.

As for Sky—I knew from the beginning that she would be a kick-ass heroine. My favorite thing about these two is their banter and how they come to respect one another even though they clash.

As with most projects I do, I started this with the intent of one book, but then the other characters started stealing the limelight, and now Wolffe Peak is a place I hope to return to again and again. Thank you for being a part of this book.

Gwen

# ACKNOWLEDGMENTS

Thanks go to my editor, Jennifer Moorman for her time and knowledge, and my buddies and beta-readers T. Breau, R.E. Butler, J. Dodge, E. Grover, D. Herbert, and K. Lambson. Cover by CT Covers Creations.

*For my husband...*

*She is his one desire...*

Werewolf Skylar Callahan turned her back on everything she held dear in search of a career. Now a public advocate for her own kind, her political ambitions have shot her straight to the top. But amidst the glitz and glamour lurks a dark presence, one who is obsessed with claiming Skylar as his own. To survive, she must rely on Wyatt Turner—a sexy, albeit lethal, alpha who insists everything be done his way.

*He is the only one who can love her...*

Wyatt is always looking to stir up trouble, and Skylar is trouble with a capital T. Not only has his wolf chosen her as his intended mate, but she also comes with her very own stalker. Consumed by his need to protect her, Wyatt doesn't care that she's determined to keep him at arm's length. It's his job to keep her safe, which means getting close to the stubborn she-wolf...just the way he wants it.

# PROLOGUE

Skylar Callahan's house was quiet.

His heavy steps were the only sound within the small, deserted house. From the waning scent, he'd wager she'd been gone a couple of weeks. He caressed faded pictures trapped within their frames and made his way up the winding staircase, his nose leading him toward her bedroom. With every step, he burned the layout into his memory, such as the low groan he heard when he placed his weight on the third stair, and the feel of the rough banister, unstable beneath his hand. This was the only place he could connect with her—the only place he felt a semblance of sanity return to him. Here, he could remember who he was.

At the top of the stairs, he paused in her bedroom doorway and cast a longing glance over her possessions. Her bedspread lay rumpled, her pillow askew from when she'd last slept here. Other signs of her presence were a small, folded pile of clothing placed carefully atop an oaken desk, and a cluttered stack of reports brimming with charming scribbles that brought an ache to his chest.

With a stuttered breath, he crossed the room and plucked a thin scrap of material from the foot of her bed. Soft and silky, the shift pooled over his fingers. He lifted her satin lingerie to his face and inhaled, his lashes shuttering when he caught a whiff of her delicate scent. A shiver rippled down his spine, and his beast growled from deep within his body. His wolf *knew* that Skylar was his mate, the only one ever meant for him. Except, he'd never mustered the courage to claim her, a mistake he would never again make.

For a moment, he imagined her here with him. He opened his eyes and stared at her bed, picturing her spread bare before him, her thighs parted as she welcomed him. Warmth shot through his stomach as he envisioned crossing the room and taking her. Her cheeks would flush as he brought her to the brink of pleasure again and again. Her sweet lips would whisper filthy words as she told him exactly what she wanted him to do. Her legs would grip his waist, urging him faster...

With Sky, there would be nothing but pure rapture. He'd wanted her for so long but had never seen his dream fulfilled. The image of her alight in his head was radiant and strong. His hand drifted down the length of his body and rubbed the satin over the hard ridge in his jeans. Biting back a moan, pleasure punched through him as he slid down his zipper and wrapped the slip around his throbbing erection.

*No. Not like this.* He sucked in a shuddering breath and corrected himself before turning from the room. No, he had something *much* better in mind. Why rely on his palm when he had the real thing in the next room? Lost to his fantasies, he'd nearly forgotten about his companion.

As he moved down the hallway, soft whimpers rose from the other side of a door. He slapped it open, and a flood of light illuminated the woman he'd dragged here. Wheat-colored locks matted her brow, her hair a match to Sky's. When he'd first laid eyes on this beauty, he'd been convinced it *was* Sky. It wasn't until she'd turned that he'd realized this bitch was nothing more than any other slut, offering it up for free to any man who would have her. It hadn't stopped him though. Her hair was the right color, and though her eyes were the wrong shade of blue, he needed only to pluck them out—an urge he felt rise when she turned up a tearful gaze.

He crouched before her and slipped a finger under her gag, drawing it down over her chin. His beast awoke at the sight of her, its ears pinned back. *Not her.* He soothed his wolf. He was well aware that this bitch wasn't Sky. But after so much searching, he needed a release.

"Please..." Her mouth was wet with tears, her plea a plaintive wail. A flash of annoyance whipped through him. Human. Dark blue eyes. Wrong scent. This wasn't right. Nothing was right. But he would make it right.

"Shh." He cupped her cheek and flashed a predatory grin that made her gasp.

Shoulders tight, she pushed away from him until her back met the wall.

"Put this on." He pulled her to her feet and placed

the thin slip in her palm. "I want you to look beautiful for me, Sky."

Wide sapphire eyes darted to his. He wanted to stab them out. "I'm not Sky. Please, don't do this."

He knew she wasn't Sky, but he needed to appease his beast, tame the rage within that burned for her. "Put it on."

Her bottom lip trembled, but finally, she submitted. Heart skipping in his chest, he stepped back. She closed her eyes and gave a weak moan before she plucked at her wrinkled shirt and lifted it slowly over her head. When her blonde hair spilled over the edge of the material, he sucked in a sharp breath. *Sky...finally.*

She glanced away from him, her arms covering her chest. *No, that won't do.* He wanted to see her nipples harden, wanted to taste them through the delicate material. Stepping forward, he laced their fingers together and dragged her to Sky's bedroom. Docile and terrified, she trailed after him, too frightened to disobey.

"There," he grunted, pointing at the bed. "Remove your bottoms and get on the bed."

She whimpered, visibly crumpling at the sight of the mattress.

He pushed her forward, a deep growl rumbling low in his chest when she cast a final glance over her shoulder. The bed shifted beneath her weight, and the moment she swung her pale legs up, he groaned and staggered toward her.

This was it. The moment he'd craved for so long. Quivering fingers slid under the lip of her thong, and his cock jumped. He felt like a horny teenager about to

4

experience his first time. As she shimmied them down her legs, he stumbled to the edge of the bed and sank to his knees.

His sweet Sky. His fingers gripped her inner thighs and prised them apart, exactly as he'd always imagined.

"Please, I'm not Sky," she sobbed. "Let me go. I won't tell anyone."

His wolf snapped at the thought of releasing her. This was Sky's bed—their dream was so close to being realized. And though deep within he knew this woman would never be her, his mind assured him she would suffice. It was a realization that filled him with bliss as he shucked his own clothing.

The moment he touched her, a fog settled over his thoughts. Silky skin, firm breasts, tight ass... Moments of bliss stole his mind, but then came anger and frustration when she wouldn't willingly give herself to him.

This wasn't right. She wasn't Sky. He lost himself, his rage taking hold. Claws sprouted from his hands, and he raked the sharp daggers down her front, shredding her into thin ribbons. She jerked in shock, and he watched with dead eyes as crimson sluiced over her ivory skin.

She grew quiet, the fight in her vanishing as blood stained her supple breasts.

This wasn't what he wanted. And it was all *her* fault.

The fog lifted and he stared down at the woman. Her wrong eyes stared back, darker, accusing, and dead. Not her. *Not her.* But it could be. He only needed to find her.

Then she would love him.

# 1

Wyatt Turner crouched by the edge of a rock enclosure, the lip of his leather boots digging into his shins. If he cocked his head just right, he could see a small female discarded at the bottom of the gorge, torn to shreds. Pale blonde hair caught the light of the burning sun and a haloed glow encircled her ruined body.

With a sigh, he pushed his sunglasses up into his hair and stared down the distance. The rank stench of death slapped him in the face, as did the crisp scent of autumn and a dried creek bed. From his limited view, he'd wager the enclosure had kept her body protected from the elements, but the scavengers would find her if the local police didn't reach her soon.

"Heartbreaking, ain't it?"

Wyatt tensed before he replaced his sunglasses and lifted his narrowed gaze. Of course, James Griffon had made an appearance. The man was infamous for chasing any story he deemed sensational, all with the hope of making a name for himself.

Jaw tight, Wyatt attempted to smooth the anger from his face. "Don't you have anything better to do than visit dead women?"

James lifted his camera and hid behind the viewfinder. Seconds later, a flash refracted off Wyatt's tinted lenses. "Perfect. What a great shot of the local alpha investigating the latest killing. She was done in by a werewolf, eh? That's why you're here? Don't growl at me, the public has a right to know what monsters they live among."

With a curled lip, Wyatt pushed to his feet and glared at the pathetic excuse of a man. "Why don't you take your little camera and skedaddle? You're in over your head, Mr. Griffon."

"Little camera?" James huffed a bitter laugh. "This *little* camera is worth more than most people's salaries."

"Then it would be a shame to see it smashed against the rock." Wyatt gave a half-shrug. "Accidents have been known to happen, you know."

The camera lowered a fraction, and Wyatt met the reporter's stare. "Is that a threat, Alpha?"

Wyatt tugged his sunglasses down the bridge of his nose and offered a toothy grin. Pushy humans—always searching for something, always causing trouble. "You should know better than that, James. I don't threaten. But it is awfully rocky around here. I'd hate for you to trip and break your toy. Or worse...your neck. So, why don't you head on out before those officers over there turn away and I grow tired of your antics? I'm sure they'll release the information to the public as soon as they can."

Abrasive laughter exploded from James' lips. "I'm here for the *truth*, Alpha. Not to pander whatever story the sheriff's office comes up with."

"Are you suggesting they'd lie?"

"All I'm saying is I want the truth."

"If you don't get that camera out of my face in the next second, you're going to be walking funny for the next year."

James snorted, though fear shadowed his face. "The public has a right to know. Haven't you noticed the similarities? This is the third murder in less than six months. All blonde and blue-eyed, all the same height and build."

The third? That was news to him. "I appreciate the lesson, Mr. Griffon. But this has nothing to do with my pack. There are a great deal of monsters in the world without pointing a finger at werewolves."

"Maybe not, but serial killers don't normally possess superhuman strength or senses. I think the public is going to appreciate being warned about this sicko."

Wyatt's neck coiled. The human didn't realize how close to death he was. As the alpha of the Colorado River Basin Pack, his most important duty was to protect his people. He'd given the snivelling reporter a chance once before, only for him to breach the pack's trust and run a story about their personal lives. Wyatt would not be so forgiving again. "You print that and next time we meet, it won't be in front of the local police."

James threw up his hands. "What do you want from me, Wyatt?"

He ignored the blatant insult. "To let us do our jobs."

"Right." James stepped closer, unaware of Wyatt's stiffening shoulders. "It's my job to expose the truth. Yours is to wrangle in those hellions you call your pack and ensure they leave us poor humans be. Theirs," he jabbed a finger toward the police, "is to ensure the safety of the public. I'm the only one doing my job."

Wyatt ran a rough hand down his warm face. He loathed humans, and James Griffon was at the top of his list. "Let them do their job—"

Another burst of laughter. The sound was beginning to grate against his nerves. "You need to give me something, Alpha. Or I'm running the story with the headline *Werewolf Serial Killer.*"

Wyatt simmered with rage. The gall of this dickhead, to boldly blackmail him, as though he was nothing more than a pup who could be intimidated. He pushed into James' space and glared down on the pitiful human. "Leave. Or I'll show you what a real werewolf looks like."

James paled and shrank backward. "I'm only saying—"

"Oh, I heard you loud and clear. You've crossed a line, Griffon."

"Alpha—"

James fell silent the moment Wyatt's fingers curled around the camera. He gave the slightest flex, and the plastic body caved in his palm.

The reporter's mouth gaped as he stared at the mess that was once his camera. "You son-of-a—"

Wyatt's lip curled. He drew his sunglasses down and unleashed his glare upon the man. "Care to finish that?"

His mouth snapped shut with a click.

"This woman deserves the full attention of the police," Wyatt growled. "Not some gossip-hungry peddler circling her like a starving vulture. Make a name for yourself somewhere else, Mr. Griffon."

Wyatt held his gaze, his amusement rising at the sight of James' discomfort. Finally, he stomped away, all the while muttering under his breath about bullies and dickhead werewolves who'd get their comeuppance.

"Well?"

Once Wyatt had his wolf reigned in, he turned to face Sheriff Shane Carlton, whose gaze tracked James as he stormed away. Clearly, Wyatt wasn't the only one concerned about the reporter's presence here. The last thing they needed was an article hitting the Web about a werewolf serial killer unleashed upon the public.

"I need to get closer to the body. At this point, the only scent I'm picking up is death."

Shane grimaced. "You can smell that?"

Wyatt hummed an affirmation.

"I'm afraid I can't accommodate that." Disapproval turned down Shane's mouth. "As much as I would love to, the medical examiner gets first poke at the body."

The body. How quickly the young woman had turned into something else. "Mr. Griffon mentioned this is the third woman. That true?"

Shane grunted. "Friggin' reporters and their big mouths. We're trying to keep that quiet."

"You're trying to keep quiet that there's a new serial killer on the loose? Does that seem wise?"

The sheriff dragged a hand down his face. His discomfort was as plain as the day was bright. "Listen, before we run around town screaming wolf—" He winced. "No offense."

"Some taken."

"—we need more information."

A sharp scent hit Wyatt's nose. Pushing his sunglasses into his hair, he turned and scratched the ridge of his nose. "You know, there's something you should know about werewolves, Sheriff."

"And what's that?"

"We can smell when someone isn't being truthful."

Shane sucked in a breath. "Are you accusing me of lying?"

"You betcha." He tapped his nose. "It's never steered me wrong."

Before his eyes, the sheriff wilted. He dug a handkerchief from his back pocket and mopped the sweat from his brow.

"When I offered my services to the local law enforcement, it was with the understanding that they would be honest with me. How can you expect me to trust you if—"

"All right," Shane hissed. "*Yes*, this is the third body. There, are you happy?"

"Not particularly. Why wasn't I called in for the other two?"

The sheriff speared Wyatt with a glare. "I appreciate

your offer to assist with any werewolf-related cases, I really do."

"But?"

Shake shrugged. "You're not a cop."

There was more to the story, and though Wyatt was prepared to demand the information, the sheriff wasn't one to be bullied, nor would he try. The relations between the werewolves and humans had been strained since they'd announced their presence to the world more than a decade ago. As a means of tackling the divide, Wyatt had offered himself to the local police, should the need ever arise. They'd never had a reason to take him up on his offer, until now.

"Well, standing up here isn't doing us any good. I need to get down there. Your perp may have left something I can use to ID him."

Shane chuckled. "*Perp*. Already learning the lingo, I see. Next you'll be applying to be a deputy."

Wyatt grunted. Fat chance of that ever happening. He might have offered his services to the local police, but that hardly meant he liked them.

"Our medical examiner is pulling in. If she clears you to go down with her, I'll allow it."

Wyatt nodded, then rocked back on his heels and let his gaze roam the rich landscape as his thoughts meandered. Without another word, the sheriff loped off to greet a well-dressed woman, whom he could only assume was the medical examiner. He eyed her lush curves beneath her pleated suit, his mouth tugging at the corner.

"Wyatt Turner, this is Dr. Elizabeth Morrison. Elizabeth, this is Wyatt, our resident alpha."

Dark brown eyes assessed him, her mouth a grim line. "Shane informs you that you would like to come down with me."

"If you want to know who did this or not, then I need to go down."

Shane and Elizabeth shared a glance. "Sheriff?"

He shrugged. "If it's the same unsub as the last one, the DNA tests will prove it."

"I'm sorry, *unsub*?" Wyatt questioned.

"Unidentified subject," Dr. Morrison confirmed without glancing at him.

"But if Wyatt can pick up a scent and track it—"

Wyatt's mouth twisted. "I'm not a fucking bloodhound." Nor would he hand one of his own over to the local police. Werewolves had their own laws to abide by.

Elizabeth swung back around, her nose scrunching as her gaze raked his length. "All right. I'll take you down with me. But know this, I don't care if you're an alpha. You do as I say, got it?"

Wyatt unleashed the brunt of his stare on the overbearing woman before him. He loosened his hold on his wolf and allowed the beast to peek out of his eyes, long enough for the color to blanch from the medical examiner's face. "Whatever you say, princess."

Rage colored her neck. "I don't think you understand—"

"Nor do I care," he informed her. "Alpha means I

don't play the role of lackey. I'll take *you* down with *me*, and you'll do as I say."

Fury flashed through her eyes. "Excuse me?"

"Uh, guys?" Shane muttered as he stepped between them.

Without warning, Wyatt strode toward the edge of the gorge and dropped over the side without a rope.

"Mr. Turner!"

The medical examiner's face was the first to pop over the edge. Chuckling to himself, Wyatt shrugged. "Any moment now, Doc."

From above came the sound of urgent curses as she slid into her required safety gear. Wyatt took the opportunity to investigate the body before anyone else rappelled down. At first glance, he knew the woman hadn't been killed here. A brutal attack such as hers tended to leave evidence, of which there was little. The bitter stench of death attacked his nose, but missing from it was the coppery tang of blood. Their victim had been moved after death.

From above, he'd seen the garish marks that marred her torso. Down here, there was no doubt in his mind what creature could have made such a gash. Werewolf claws were thicker and longer than a bear's. These gouges were bone deep, and most certainly not from a bear. Fortunately for his pack, the scent wasn't one he knew.

Wyatt studied the poor woman, his attention coming to rest on her face.

*Sweet Lord.*

He'd seen some disturbing things in his life, but the two gaping holes staring back at him rendered him silent.

The fucker had cut out her eyes. Wyatt cursed and whipped a hand through his hair as he thought about the repercussions.

It seemed James had been correct, after all, and as the only alpha in the state, the responsibility would fall on Wyatt to find this psycho.

*Yeehaw.*

## 2

He was watching her again.

Sky knew the moment his gaze settled on her; she felt a menacing chill lift the hairs on the back of her neck. And no, the chill had nothing to do with the autumn wind that had picked up as she'd vacated the cab. It was *him*.

At first, everything had felt fine, but after a few minutes, her inner wolf had pricked up her ears, her stance deadly alert. As an innate hunter, she recognized when she became prey.

The moment her plane had touched down, she'd phoned Shane—exactly as the sheriff had insisted—but he'd asked her to wait until he could send a patrol car for her. That idea hadn't sat well with her. She wanted her home, her bed, and her bathtub. A long, hot soak was exactly what she needed. So, when the cabbie flicked off his light, she'd hopped in.

She shouldn't have left the cab, not when she knew there was a madman after her, but all she'd wanted was to return home after a particularly exhausting week away. It wasn't the cabbie's fault he'd driven over glass, or that the tire had popped. These things happened. And even with a stalker on the loose, she should have been safe for the twenty minutes it would have taken her to walk home. Except, like everything else in her life, even this simple task had gone awry.

She drew in a deep breath, but the blustery wind whisked up a plethora of scents that overwhelmed her nose. Thankfully, she could still hear, and there in the distance were footsteps wading through the dead leaves. The crunch of his steps echoed her own, as they had for the past six blocks. Though her heart raced forward, she managed to maintain an even pace. *Keep calm*, as the mantra said. Could be a friendly pedestrian out for a nighttime walk...down the same paths that she was headed, without any deviation. *Right.*

A gust of air swirled around her, and riding the current was the recognizable stench of fur and forest. The same scent that had haunted her for the past year. It seemed no matter where she went, there *he* was. Always in the distance, taunting her.

In the beginning, she'd refused to admit that she was being stalked. She'd thrown away the first letters and silenced the calls in an attempt to assure herself that they were pranks. Even after she'd finally sought out the cops, it'd taken Shane weeks to convince her that there was someone out there who was obsessed with her.

Sky stiffened as a shiver rippled down her spine. She still felt his eyes on her, heard his careful steps as he breached the distance between them. Once upon a time, she hadn't feared other werewolves—hell, her job was to *advocate* for them—but life had a way of kicking someone down. It made campaigning for her own kind difficult when one of them had turned her into prey.

Shaking off the terror, she scoped her surroundings, dismayed to find the moonlit streets abandoned. Two blocks north, a large van sat on the curb. It would only provide her a couple seconds of a lead, but that was all she needed.

She counted her breaths as she went, careful to keep them steady. The moment she slipped behind the van, she bolted. For a brief moment, she thought he hadn't followed, but the sound of his quick footfalls assured her otherwise. Sky kept her eyes forward as she measured her follower's pace, hopeful the distance between them would grow.

It didn't.

Her heart fluttered with panic. His steps grew louder, his breaths uneven as he closed the distance between them. A whimper slipped from her lips as she skidded around the next corner, fingers digging into the brick wall for purchase.

Fear had led her in the wrong direction. Eyes wide, she cursed at the sight of the large park ahead of her. Hardly the best place to escape someone. She feared her only option was to shift. Humans knew of werewolves, but it wasn't recommended to take wolf form in the middle of the street—public indecency and all that. Not to mention that most humans felt they had the right to hunt any beasts that crossed onto their property, and Sky loathed the idea of her skin hung on a hunter's wall.

But what other option did she have?

By her estimation, her pursuer had closed half the distance. She listened to the sound of his strained breaths, yet his pace never wavered.

For the first time, she braved glancing back.

A monstrous shadow rushed after her. Even with her heightened sense of sight, she saw nothing beyond his height and build. She contemplated shifting in the middle of the street, but the time it would take to change would cost her everything.

So she did the only other thing she could think of. "Help!"

His stride faltered and a slight hitch carried to her ears.

Sky repeated her plea while dashing toward the park. "Somebody, help!"

Not that there was anyone around to assist, but her outburst had gained her a few spare moments. While her pursuer stumbled over his steps and debated whether or not to continue the chase, she shucked her clothing and let her frightened wolf take over. Fear hastened her shift. Fur sprouted from her skin as her bones cracked and reshaped.

Nails skittering against the pavement, she kicked off the last leg of her jeans and raced forward once more. Another curse zinged through the air as her pursuer realized what she'd done.

The distance between them grew with every stride until she could no longer hear him. Still, she continued to bark for help. If the humans refused to answer, perhaps someone of her kind would. She tore through the secluded woods, zipping around trees and ruffling piles of leaves, all while howling at the top of her lungs.

A final glance back revealed her success. The only shadows were those of the park. Heart in her throat, she turned, her chest heaving as she struggled to slow her breath. She'd done it. Thank goodness.

Jubilant, she did a quick circle and chuffed her pleasure. Whoever had been following her was long gone. If only she could fist pump the air. Instead, she contented herself with a happy yip. She didn't care that she'd lost an entire outfit along the way, she'd replace every article.

With her tail held high, she turned to continue a light jog home when a large fist grasped her by the scruff and yanked her into the air.

Terror squeezed her heart. Firm digits gripped her and dangled her five feet above the ground as though her weight was no concern.

With a panicked breath, she squeezed her eyes shut and lashed out, kicking with all four paws while snapping her teeth. She couldn't have cared less what she bit, so long as her captor released her.

The moment her teeth sank into an arm, she rejoiced and dug in until blood gushed into her mouth.

"Jesus H. Christ, woman!" A savage growl rent the night air.

Sky's heart slammed against her ribs, but rather than release her target, she clamped her jaws down and shook her head like a dog. Her muscles tensed as she awaited retaliation. Instead, her feet continued to dangle, the fingers in her scruff holding tight.

"Are you finished?" came a deep voice.

Sky cracked open an eyelid and peered up from beneath her eyelashes at the scowling giant who held her hostage. She popped open her other eye and let her gaze sweep up his leather-clad length.

*Oh, crap!*

Swallowing past the searing blood, Sky unlatched her jaw and released the burly arm from her mouth. Now she was in for it. Though she hadn't caught a glance of her attacker's face, she highly doubted the alpha of the Colorado River Basin Pack had been the one following her. Though his scent possessed a familiar note of fur, it wasn't the same as the one who stalked her. She swallowed and braced herself before meeting the alpha's furious gaze.

"I'm going to release you, now." His jaw ticked his displeasure. "If you run, I will hunt you down."

Sky swallowed a slight squeak. Running was what she did best, but rather than test him, she nodded and braced for the slight drop. Instead, he lowered her gently, waiting for all fours to touch the concrete before releasing his grip on her scruff.

"Shift."

One word, yet she knew this was more than a request. Her bones complied before her mind did, and she groaned as her body crumpled. The shift came slower, her wolf howling in her head the entire time. *Run!* They weren't safe until they were behind locked doors.

But she couldn't. The alpha had warned her of the repercussions if she did. Not to mention that she was too exhausted to shift again so quickly, and outrunning him on two legs didn't seem possible.

With a wavering breath, she pushed to her feet with a grunt, her lashes fluttering as she staggered to the side. No helping hands came from the alpha; instead, Sky gripped the nearest tree until the dizziness passed. Only then did she open her eyes.

The alpha stood across from her, blood slowly seeping from his injured arm as he leaned against a lamppost. Ambient light shone down on him, illuminating his massive frame, slate eyes, and rigid jaw. At first glance, Wyatt Turner was a truly frightening man. Every inch of him was hardened muscle, as though he made it a personal goal to maintain zero body fat, something most would have killed for. Truthfully, though, his fit frame had more to do with his rough-and-tumble lifestyle as did the jagged scar that began at the corner of his mouth and slashed across his cheek. Or so her dossier claimed. It was her job to know the many alphas scattered around the country—and Wyatt was not someone easily forgotten.

Her gaze raked over the terrifying scar. She couldn't recall its history, nor could she tear her eyes away from it. In the amber light, it stood in stark relief, highlighting the unnatural crook of his mouth. Another scar severed the edge of his right eyebrow, though his eye remained untouched. He was one bad-ass mofo, his extraordinary frame hugged by the finest leathers.

He cocked a thick brow and studied her, the slight

twitch in his wide jaw the only indication that his arm ached. "Explain."

Skylar's nerves fluttered in her stomach and she gazed back the way she'd come. Nothing. For all intents and purposes, the park appeared abandoned. Her nostrils flared as she drew in a breath—still nothing. But she knew the truth. She'd felt the chill deep down in her bones. *He'd* been here.

The alpha cleared his throat.

Sky turned back to him, an embarrassed blush chasing over her cheeks. Like she wanted to admit to an alpha that she'd run from a threat. No werewolf worth a grain of salt would have acted in such a way, but it wasn't as though it was a human stalking her. It rankled her to no end that she'd run, but her stalker was a full-blooded male werewolf. What chance did she stand in a fight?

"I—I know it isn't recommended to shift in city limits," she stuttered as she gazed down her bare length. Thankfully, nudity was a regular occurrence in the daily routine of a werewolf.

"So, you thought you'd run around howling for shits and giggles? Doesn't explain why you reek of fear or," he held up his arm, "this."

Sky blew out a harsh breath. "I was being followed, all right?"

The other brow winged up, and the alpha pushed off the lamppost. He strode toward her, his muscles bunching beneath the leather as he moved, and drew in a deep breath. She knew what scents he'd find—moss, grass, dead leaves—nothing that indicated the presence of anyone other than them.

A flicker of skepticism darkened his eyes. "No one here but you and me."

Her mouth twisted and she let her gaze sweep his length, taking in the dark blue jeans that peeked out from beneath his chaps and the black T-shirt stretched across his chest. It was true—it was only the two of them... Fear punched through her gut. Surely, that couldn't mean Wyatt had been the one following her, could it? She knew there were alphas who could mask or change their scent, but he couldn't have been the one stalking her. Though...she recalled the shadowed image of the brute that had chased her through the streets, and she realized with a jolt of fear that Wyatt was the right height and build.

Before she could speak on her behalf, Wyatt stepped over the path and approached her. Sky's breath caught, the sheer size of him pushing her back a step. His hand reached out, and she watched with a parted mouth as he grasped a strand of her hair and wrapped it around his index finger.

"Blonde," he stated, his mouth pursed as though her hair color offended him. His gaze drilled into hers as he grabbed her chin and forced her head up. "Blue eyes."

Her heart shot up into her throat. Had her assessment of Wyatt Turner been wrong? His scent was different! But her wolf scolded her for basing her impression off such an inane thing. She knew what alphas were capable of! Sky went still, her blood like ice as she faced who she now believed to be her stalker. *Fight*, her wolf howled in her head.

The alpha leaned in, and when he drew in her scent,

she snapped her knee up, drilling him in his tender bits before she turned and fled.

**3**

---

S *weet Jesus, Mary, and Joseph.*

Wyatt groaned and staggered for the nearest tree, the air rushing from his lungs. It'd been years since anyone had dared sack him. And while he wanted nothing more than to drop to his knees and pray to the heavens above that his boys still dangled from the appropriate spot, he couldn't allow the she-wolf to escape.

So he stood straight, shook off the blow, and raced forward, his stride a little bowlegged thanks to that sharp knee. What he hadn't expected was to have to sprint to keep up with her, quick-footed little minx that she was. Nor had he expected a small smile to tug at his lips as he watched her firm ass book it through the mossy trees. Stark naked, and that hardly slowed her. Someone had eaten her Wheaties. 'Course, he had to remember that the little devil had attacked him and disobeyed his order. He mustn't forget that.

But if he didn't catch her soon—preferably before she bolted out into the streets—there'd be a hefty indecent exposure ticket coming her way. A shame, really. Anyone with such a pert ass should be able to flaunt it as much as she liked.

As he watched her duck around a carved tree stump, he wondered if she'd been the next intended victim. Blonde and blue-eyed, after all. Which may not have been a requirement, but three dead bodies with matching physical characteristics was more than coincidence. And if she was the next mark, it raised another question: were any of the others werewolves? He'd only seen the one victim from today, and she was human. Shane had agreed to let him look at the files for the other two, so he made a mental note to research that. This one, though, had the sweet smell of werewolf all over her. The moment he'd lifted her in the air, he'd felt it settle into his lungs—a mouth-watering combination of fur, forest, and a whiff of honeysuckle.

He hopped over the same stump, fingers tearing at his clothes as he moved, before shifting midair. As alpha, it was a move he'd perfected years ago. And with his bulk, it was the only way he would catch her. Tiny thing that she was, she zipped through the coppice, narrowly avoiding the grasping branches that seemed determined to make his life miserable.

Wyatt ate up the distance between them without trying. He dogged her steps, waiting for the upcoming bed of moss before launching into the air and taking her down. Her sharp squeal of terror cut straight through his chest. At the last moment, he tucked his paws so as not to scratch her. Except, the little spitfire took the opportunity to throw a right hook.

*Stars...*

Sparkly lights danced before his eyes, his jaw aching. Christ. He shook his head and slapped her arms down with his front paws, bracing her weight as she squirmed against him. Vocabulary would be useful here. But first he snapped his teeth in her face, his lips reared back, revealing his fangs to ensure she got the point. Face pale, her bottom lip trembled...and oh hell, didn't that slay him. His heart squeezed at the sight of a single tear slipping down her cheek. With a sigh, he lowered his lips and shifted, his paws lengthening into strong fingers that held her pinned.

"Please," she whispered.

Wyatt groaned, trying to ignore the sensation of her brushing against him. "Would you stop?" he hissed. Because hell if his dick wasn't responding to her small thrusts, the traitorous bastard.

"Let me go," she pleaded. "I won't tell anyone. I—"

"Woman," Wyatt growled, "if you'd just listen..."

She stilled beneath him, a strange twinkle in her eyes.

Wyatt's brows deepened. What schemes did she have running through her head? "I'm not going to—"

*Pain.*

Wyatt groaned. It took every ounce of strength to hold her down and not fall to the side. Where the hell had she learned to headbutt someone like that? For the third time tonight, he shook himself and struggled to clear away the tiny, twittering birds that fluttered around his head.

"—hurt you," he grunted.

"W—What?"

Oh, thank the Lord. "I said..." He released one of her arms to lift a hand to his head. He couldn't believe this teeny woman had nearly knocked him out cold. Some alpha. "I'm not going to hurt you."

"Then why did you chase me?" Her warm breath brushed over his mouth.

"Why did you sack me?"

She shifted her weight for a second time, that knee in question accidentally brushing against him. Wyatt sucked in a sharp breath and snapped his jaw shut, blindsided by a confusing cocktail of pain and pleasure.

"No, why were you chasing me before that?"

"Before what?" He wanted to bat at the offending birds that still circled his head. Couldn't think with them up there, whistling Dixie as they went round and round and round.

"Back on the street!" She wriggled her other arm free and pushed up onto her elbows.

Wyatt's gaze dropped. Oh buddy, don't look there. Not that he could tear his gaze away now that he'd succumbed. Two small mounds stared up at him, and much like the proverbial cherry on top, her nipples were deliciously taut. From the cold, you sick pervert. Snarling at himself, he forced his gaze northward, his mouth twisting at the sheer annoyance in her eyes. "I wasn't chasing you on the street."

She pursed her lush pink lips. "That wasn't you?"

"Sweetheart, as you can see, I don't chase. I catch."

Anger bloomed within her, the sharp scent smacking him in his face. And hell if it wasn't enticing—like a splash of spice mixed with something sweet. "Get off me."

He spared a glance down their lengths and dropped his head at the sight of his not-so-little soldier standing at full attention. Uh...

"Now, if you don't mind."

Wyatt lifted his head and glared down on her until she flinched. Like hell he was going to take orders from a sprite of a thing, trapped beneath him. "Talk," he said, resorting to his infamous one-worded orders.

"About?"

He pulled his lips back in a savage snarl. She knew exactly what explanation he wanted—playing coy wasn't going to solve matters.

With a long sigh, she collapsed back into the undergrowth and stared up at the canopy as defeat chased across her face. "There's nothing to explain. I was being followed, so I ran."

"Really." He held her stare, waiting for her to elaborate.

She pushed her long tresses back from her face, her nose wrinkled as she gazed up into the midnight sky. Seemed she was hell bent on ignoring him. A deep growl built up in Wyatt's throat. People didn't ignore him. They stood at attention and obeyed. Hence, alpha. But this little spitfire refused to look at him, let alone listen.

"Care to elaborate?"

She dropped her chin and pinned him with a frustrated stare that raised his hackles. "Why?"

"Why?" Wyatt blinked. What the... No one ever questioned him.

"Look, this really isn't any of your business, 'kay? So, get off me."

The growl rumbled out of his throat.

"Please?" she asked with a quirked mouth, as though placating him.

"Tell ya what." Wyatt settled down onto his elbows, his clasped hands hovering above her teasingly gorgeous breasts. "We're going to stay right here, in this exact position, until you spill the beans."

"What?" she shrieked.

Wyatt lifted his brows. "I'm not kidding."

"Look, I don't know who he is!" she finally exclaimed. "But I do know I'm being watched, all right? Everywhere I go, I feel his eyes on me."

"Whose?"

"His!" she shouted. "I don't know who. I know how this sounds. But I'm telling the truth."

The truth about what? So far he hadn't gotten anything of value out of her.

"Can I go now?" she mumbled, clearly annoyed with the topic of conversation.

Wyatt almost laughed. "Sure, darling."

Her eyes shot open and she gazed up at him with a look of such wonder. "Really?"

"No."

Her face crumpled. "I'm sorry I attacked you! I thought..."

"What did you think?"

"It doesn't matter." She raked her hands down her face and blew out a heavy breath.

"My balls disagree."

She sucked in her bottom lip and shot a glance down. At the sight of him hovering above her, she swallowed and flicked him a wary glance. Because that was what a man loved to see, sheer panic at the sight of his dick. He refused to apologize for it; he was hovering above an attractive woman—gorgeous, actually—and the cock wants what the cock wants.

"What's your name?" he finally demanded. There were other answers he needed as well, like what the hell she was doing so close to his territory because he knew she wasn't one of his. No way would he have been able to keep his hands off her if she were. For now, though, he'd settle for her name.

Her tongue flicked out and dampened her lips. And there went the rest of his blood. "Skylar. Sky Callahan."

He frowned. Why was her name so familiar? But rather than ask, he pushed to his feet and turned away. "Get up."

"Uh, where are we going?"

Wyatt glanced over his shoulder. It was his heart that stirred this time, contracting at the sight of her meek and terrified, kneeling in the soft moonlight. Clearing his throat, he jerked his head in the direction they'd come. Keep your head on straight, boyo. No time to let the libido steal the show. "Now." He refused to wait; instead, he turned and stalked back into the thick brush.

---

*Don't cry.*

Skylar forced her lower lip still—tears wouldn't gain her anything. Nor would the werewolf stalking through the brush ahead of her appreciate them. She'd felt how he'd tensed above her when a single tear had escaped. To their kind, strength and ferocity was revered, something Wyatt Turner possessed in spades. Snivelling over the delicate position she'd landed herself in wouldn't endear her to anyone.

Not that she wanted to endear herself to him. Unfortunately for Sky, anger and fear weren't emotions she handled well. For some reason, they always resulted in tears. And right now she was both terrified and furious. At him for thinking he could control her, at herself for allowing it, and terrified because she'd thought he was going to kill her.

Still, the last thing she wanted was to appear weak. For the past decade, she'd lived amongst humans and had picked up certain trademarks that she knew her kind wouldn't take well to. She couldn't imagine what he thought of her right now, a discomfiting thought that brought a curse to her lips.

In her time with her former pack, she'd learned that dominant werewolves possessed an instinctive need to protect those weaker than them. And baby, Wyatt Turner was all kinds of dominant. If there was one thing she appreciated about human males, they at least tried to control their inner caveman. Werewolves, however, were incapable of separating themselves from that side.

Of course, this train of thought only served to remind her that there was something she required protection from. She'd be a fool to deny it. Whoever was stalking her, he refused to keep his obsession a secret. Nothing like a few skin-crawling letters to make a girl feel wanted.

Hot tears rushed up the back of her throat, but with a steadying breath, she tipped her head back and stared up at the starry sky. Stiff upper lip, 'ol girl, she mused. No use crying about it; tears wouldn't solve anything. Though she couldn't believe she'd sacked an alpha tonight. Or slugged him. Or, hell, headbutted him. Before she left her pack to pursue a career among the humans, she never would have been so brazen. The same couldn't be said for tonight. Fear might have been gnawing at her gut, but she'd refused to lie back and let some crazed stalker have his way with her.

She shivered.

"Problem?"

Wyatt's voice broke through her thoughts. Sky startled and dropped her chin, only to find a large man looming over her. Her breath hitched at the sight of him, built like a bloody brick house. Surely there were laws against someone looking that good. And yes, she'd stolen a gander or two. Or three. The wide expanse of his tattooed shoulders and chest had her gaze dipping down to his tapered waist. And there it was, brazen as all hell, an Adonis belt that put all others to shame. Really, it should be illegal. Like federal offense with twenty-to-life sort of punishment.

She blew out a breath and shoved her mussed hair back from her chilled face. Long ago, she'd learned that the Fates were bitches with a capital B. It wasn't surprising that they would see fit to drop a man like Wyatt in her lap when she felt as though she'd been dragged backward through the hedge. As though her pride wasn't rankled enough.

Shaking her head, she raked her teeth over her bottom lip. "No problem, but I should leave. You know, places to go, people to see...and all that..." Her voice trailed off, heat flushing her cheeks at the sight of his brow arching. Shane would be sick with worry for her. Not that she could call him with her phone abandoned somewhere back on the street.

"No."

Sky blinked. Just like that? No? "Excuse me?"

"No."

There was that word again. She slowly straightened, her eyes narrowed on him. "Listen here, Buddy." So to ensure that he understood, she enunciated her next words, adding a final punch to each by jabbing him in the chest with her finger. "You're not my alpha."

His mouth crooked at the corner, his gray eyes twinkling with restrained humor.

"This isn't funny!" Ire crept up the back of her neck.

"To you."

The bitter taste of fresh blood coated her tongue. It wasn't until then that she realized she'd bitten into her lip in frustration. "Look—"

And then he was walking again, blatantly ignoring her attempt to claim control of the situation. Sky snapped her mouth shut, her teeth grinding as she stalked behind him. Sadly, her anger seemed incapable of distracting her libido, because damn, the man had an ass finer than rump roast. She swallowed and forced her eyes above the belt. No good could come from allowing her gaze to drift.

"Why don't we start with you telling me who your alpha is?"

Sky snapped her eyes up, noting that comical arch of his brow as he watched her from over his shoulder. And didn't that bust her chops, getting caught scoping out his ass like a randy school girl.

"I don't have one," she grumbled.

His deep laughter echoed through the trees. "Really."

"I'll have you know that I can take care of myself. I answer to no alpha." Chin high, she made a show of ignoring him as they pressed forward.

"Ah, a feminist," he said as he continued through the foliage, his steps even and controlled.

Sky's mouth dropped. The nerve! "Just because I'm not a member of a pack doesn't make me a feminist! And say I was, what business is it of yours?" The bastard had no idea what had led her down this path, nor was she about to educate him in such matters. Her fingers clenched into a fist, and she found herself wondering if socking him in the jaw again was worth another fracture. She'd heard the crunch the moment she'd smoked him back there with her dusty right hook, but thankfully, werewolves healed fast. The bones had begun mending the moment she'd jerked back her hand.

"And who the hell do you think you are? It's none of your business—"

A warning growl cut through the trees. Sky swallowed her words, and snapped her mouth closed with a click. What the hell was she thinking, scolding an alpha like that, especially one like Wyatt? Independence didn't mean she was safe.

He turned to face her, stalking backward through the bushes, all bunched muscles and a dark tapestry of tattoos and menacing scars. "So, what does that make you, then?"

She blinked. "Huh?" Eloquent.

"If you aren't a feminist," he repeated, "then what are you?"

So, he didn't know who she was then. She shoved away the disappointment, but she should have expected as much. If she recalled correctly, Wyatt kept to himself and rarely ventured into the human world. Of course, no amount of placating soothed the sting to her ego.

Raking her hair back from her brow, she sighed. "Really tired. I want to go home, if you don't mind." Home. She hadn't set foot in her little house in more than a week. And tonight, her only intention was to snatch a few hours of sleep before she needed to leave for the airport, again. But Wyatt didn't need to know that.

"Where do you think we're going?"

*We?* She swallowed her whimper before he heard it. The last thing she wanted was to involve him. This was her problem, not his. Hell, the human police were already involved; she didn't need his help on top of it. "Uh, thanks. But I don't need an escort—"

Wyatt interrupted her with another growl, his gray eyes as dark as slate when he turned to glare at her. "You're getting one."

Her eyes fluttered shut and she sucked in a deep breath. All right. She could work with this. It wasn't as though he was going to force his way into her home and tuck her into bed. She snorted at the thought of the big bad wolf swaddling her in blankets and fluffing her pillows. Not in a million years.

"Here."

Something large and black swatted her in the face. The clean scent of soap mixed with fur filled her nose as she batted Wyatt's T-shirt away. "What in the world?"

"Put it on," he ordered as he gathered up his remaining clothes from the ground. "Then we'll go find your clothes."

Grateful for something to wear, she yanked the soft cotton down over her head as he slid into his pants. The hem reached the tips of her thighs, barely covering the lower curve of her ass. "I look ridiculous."

Wyatt lifted his head, his hard expression vanishing in the wake of something a touch more primal. With a cocked brow, Sky took a second glance, her cheeks heating at the sight of her bare legs peeking out from the dark material. All right, so maybe ridiculous wasn't the right word. And if the crook of his mouth was any indication, Wyatt didn't think so either.

Clad only in his jeans and boots, Wyatt led her through a dark labyrinth of trees, his silence unnerving. Sky secured her hair into a low knot with a thin stick, intent on asking where he was leading her, when a flash of chrome and crimson caught her eye.

"Oh no, no, no." She shook her head and kicked her heels into the lush earth. "You're insane if you think I'm getting on that thing with you."

Wyatt snaked a large hand around her waist and yanked her closer to his boldly designed motorcycle. "What's the problem?"

She shook her head, her mouth a grim line. "What's the problem? How about the fact that I'm hardly dressed! I can't plant my bare ass on your bike." She whimpered at the thought of riding behind him, her crotch pressed up against him. If ever there was a reason to be embarrassed...

"You want to go home, don't you?"

"I can walk."

His other hand cinched around her waist and held her steadfast next to the seat. "This is faster."

"Stop manhandling me! You're not going to convince me to get on that thing."

A sexy grin tugged on his scarred mouth, and, for a brief moment, Sky was stunned. The man was intimidating and powerful, and the sight of him grinning robbed her of breath. "Trust me, sweetheart. You'll know when I'm manhandling you. Let's go. I don't have all night."

She squeaked and fidgeted in his grip. "I—I don't need a ride, really. I—"

Wyatt jerked her against him with a grunt. A sharp squeal of protestation fell from Sky's lips the moment he lifted her in the air and deposited her on the back of the bike. "Stop complaining. Like I'd let you walk home alone, ass bare to the rest of the world. What kind of a bastard do you think I am?"

Before she could answer, he straddled the bike before her. The motion knocked her forward until her naked thighs cradled his. Heat rushed to her face and she wriggled backward, attempting to place a little distance between them. But then he fired up the bike, the engine roared to life, and they took off.

**4**

H e was trapped in his own personal hell.

Yup, that was the only explanation. Whatever spiritual bodies reigned on high were having the time of their lives yanking his puppet strings around. If Sky squirmed one more time, she couldn't hold him responsible for his actions. Because damn if he couldn't feel the heat of her thighs through his jeans. He'd only met the girl, but there was no denying his desire to pin her against a wall and have his way.

It didn't help that she still wore his T-shirt. Thank the Lord for the wind. If he had to smell his scent on her...his gut tightened. Worse, they hadn't been able to find any of her clothes or the bag she'd dropped mid-shift. Sky had assured him that she'd kicked her pants aside into the middle of the street. Her bra and panties might have been destroyed by the sudden shift, but she remained adamant that her other clothing had survived.

So, where were they?

Their tumble in the leaves hadn't lasted longer than ten minutes, and the streets were deserted, middle of the night as it was. There was a slight chance that someone had picked them up, but Wyatt didn't believe that. People were innately ignorant to anything that didn't involve themselves. If they saw a pair of jeans discarded in the middle of the street, they'd quirk a brow, mutter something about *kids these days*, and move on with a quick shake of their heads. Of course, there was one *other* viable option—one that disturbed him on a whole new level. Whoever had been following her had taken them. And wasn't that creepy as all fuck?

Sky's light tap on his shoulder drew his thoughts back to the present. He stole a quick glance backward to find her staring at the house at the end of the road.

"There." She mouthed the word, her finger pointed toward it.

With a nod, Wyatt geared down and came to a stop next to the curb. A quick nudge and the kickstand slipped down. Only then did he drop his hands to his thighs and stare up at the small, split-story ranch house. "This your place?"

She hopped off the bike and tugged down his shirt before nodding. "Home, sweet home."

Sweet was right. All pink trim and frilly yellow curtains fluttering in the windows, complete with a white picket fence that surrounded a stone bed full of lilies. Pink trim. Yellow curtains. Flowers. He slid her a sideways glance. Pink and yellow didn't seem her *thang*. Now, black...black was her color. His T-shirt assured him of that. Not to mention that she knew how to fight; his jaw still ached from that knuckle sandwich she'd fed him earlier. She seemed more badass than Rambo—this house did *not* fit the girl.

'Course, he could be wrong. Wouldn't be the first time. Shrugging, he started for the front door. Who was he to judge? For all he knew, this was her mother's house or something. That, or her decorator needed to be fired. 'Cuz, damn, it was like Barbie threw up all over this place.

Wyatt took two steps at a time as he climbed the stairs to the front door.

"What are you doing?" A thread of panic wove through her voice a second before her thin fingers grazed his arm.

Wyatt cocked his head and stared down at her. "Seeing you inside?" Sure, he was a tattooed Neanderthal who rode a motorcycle and ran a werewolf pack, but his momma didn't raise no fool. Everything about this little wolf screamed frightened. He wasn't leaving until he checked every last cranny in her house.

"I'm fine!" She forced a nervous laugh. "I'm sure I was imagining things."

Wyatt snorted. Pushing him away only made his decision that much clearer. Ms. Callahan was hiding something, and no amount of excuses would convince him otherwise.

"I'm going inside," he informed her. "You can either tag along or wait out here."

Rage flushed her cheeks, and *boy howdy*, if he didn't enjoy the sight of her riled up.

"No manners," she hissed, eyes pinched at the corners.

"None whatsoever. So, we doing this?"

Her head tilted back and she stared up at him with resignation in her eyes. "Do I have a choice?"

"Now you're clueing in, darling." Because, no, she didn't. Alpha meant doing what he wanted when he wanted. And what he wanted was to scope out the woman's place and find out what she was hiding. Two birds, one stone.

A growl scraped past her throat as she shoved past him and punched a number into her keyless entry. Wyatt couldn't have helped the smile that crooked his mouth even if he'd wanted to. Something about that sound amused him—like a little pup trying to make her way in the big bad world. Adorable.

He froze on her stoop and blinked. Adorable? No. There was nothing *adorable* about defiance. His mood took a foul turn. "Hurry up."

Another growl. This time, it ruffled his hackles. But he held his tongue. Now wasn't the time for a lesson in proper behaviour or protocol.

The lock clicked and Sky popped open the door.

Wyatt's lungs deflated and before either of them could step a foot within the house, he grasped her around the waist and swung her off the porch, landing in the plush grass below with her back against her house.

"What the—"

He clapped a hand over her mouth and then leaned toward her. "Shh. Don't you smell that?"

46

She rolled her eyes before mumbling, "All I smell is you."

Wyatt's gaze flicked to hers, his stomach warming with the thought of her taking in his scent. Fending off a shiver, he leaned forward until his lips brushed the shell of her chilled ear. His jaw ached with the desire to nibble on her lobe. "I'm going to remove my hand. Don't make a sound." He glanced at her once to ensure she understood. Glassy eyes met his, bright with fear. *Great.*

His fingers trailed over her lips as he drew his hand away.

She immediately scented the air. "Is that...?"

He silenced her with a sharp breath, then lifted his nose to the air. *Blood.* But more than that, the pungent stench of death slapped him in the face. Wyatt glanced down at the terrified woman pressed against his chest, trembling beyond control as she recognized the unpleasant aroma.

Someone had some 'splaining to do.

---

Sky ripped her gaze from Wyatt's and stared up at the small house that had once felt like home. Now, it was nothing. Her stalker had breached her personal sanctuary and marked it as his, like he had everything else in her life. A hot rush of tears congealed in her throat, but she swallowed them, determined to remain strong.

Wyatt set her aside and hopped back up onto the porch. "Stay here, all right? I'm going to have a look."

A beaten whimper fell past her lips. Stay out *here*? In

the dark? Alone? But he vanished into the shadows of the house before she could respond.

Sky's breath caught the moment he disappeared. The night pressed in on her until she thought she might scream. She jumped at the sound of her neighbor's rickety gate slamming shut, her hand rising to cup her throat. "Wyatt?"

A quiet sound came next, a slight *scratch*, like nails running down glass. Sky squeezed her eyes shut and backed into the side of the house, her breath lodged in her throat. What if he was out there, watching? Fear chased up her spine and forced her low into the garden. Knees tucked into her chest, she clapped her hands over her ears, if only to silence her thoughts.

She shook her head and buried her face against her legs, the sweet scent of lilies mocking her. She couldn't do this anymore. Couldn't handle the letters and phone calls. More than once, she'd changed her phone number —the house landline and her cell. Now, Shane checked and logged her messages to save her the anguish. He'd been her one steady rock in all this, and she was beyond grateful to him.

The fevered tears she'd been fighting slipped down her cheeks. She'd thought herself stronger than this. Her emergency bag sat next to her fridge, packed with everything she could think of, ready for a quick escape. All she had to do was grab it and run.

With a hiccup, Sky lifted her chin to find the doorway wide open. The house was dark-as-night, but she didn't need any light; the faint glow from the street lights would suffice. As for the alpha, she couldn't hear him at all. It was worth the risk.

Sky sucked in a tremulous breath and crept out of the lily garden on her hands and knees. One quick dash up the porch steps, snatch the bag, and then she'd be gone. Screw the alpha. It almost seemed too easy.

Her feet and hands hit the stoop and she bolted into the entryway. Her pack sat exactly where she'd left it, between the pantry and the fridge. Relief bloomed in her chest the moment her fingers latched onto the strap. One sharp tug and the bag came free.

Sky whirled on her heel and froze at the sight of a shadow hunkering in her doorway. She sucked in a deep breath and released a bloodcurdling scream.

## 5

Wyatt's heart burst from his chest at the sound of Sky's chilling shriek.

He bolted out of her bedroom and rushed down the stairs, feet clomping on each step. "Sky!"

Midway down, he heard a resounding thump, and his heart suffered another palpitation. After the scene he'd stumbled across in her bedroom, he feared what awaited him on the main floor. Gripping the stairwell, he leapt over the banister and landed in the corridor, then rushed through the living room and into the kitchen to find Sky huddled in a dark corner.

"Skylar?"

Wyatt slowed to a walk and inched toward her. The woman hardly acknowledged his presence, her gaze fixed on the wide-open doorway. That was when he scented it —the light undertone of male werewolf. He'd caught a whiff of it in her bedroom as well, hidden beneath the cloying stench of blood and death.

It seemed his first instincts had been correct. Sky was the next target.

And *damn* if his fingers didn't sprout claws at the thought.

The wolf in him demanded that he take chase and rip the sick bastard limb from limb. His lip curled with the thought. If there was one thing he couldn't abide by, it was someone preying on the weak. Not that Sky was weak. She'd proven the opposite when she'd nearly knocked his head clear off, but he couldn't abandon her to go hunting. The acrid stench of her fear burned a hole in his nose; he couldn't leave her in such a state. Not to mention that she would be vulnerable if the asshat made another attempt. The thought of staying, though, went against every bone in his body.

Hands clenched, he paced the length of the room, now and then shooting a furtive glance down at the frozen woman. The killer couldn't be picking women at random—they had to know their attacker. "Who is he, Sky?"

"I don't know."

Frustration coiled within him. He wanted this over tonight. Delaying self-gratification wasn't his thing, and the sooner he could slap a body bag around the freak, the better. "You have to know something," he growled as he stalked another lap around the kitchen. "You can't expect me to believe—"

Lurching to her feet, she stood flush against him, her head reaching his chin. "Believe what? That I would lie? The man has only made the past year of my life absolutely miserable. But, no, apparently that's something I would keep hidden!"

Wyatt arched a brow. *The past year?* There was more happening here, more than she was telling. "Well, you weren't being too forthcoming in the park, so I could only assume—"

She threw up her hands and released a frustrated grunt as she turned to stare out the kitchen window. "Excuse me for trying to protect myself."

"Protect yourself? From what? Me?"

"For starters."

*Ouch.*

She sucked in a weak breath and then a steadier one. Before his eyes, she gathered herself, and he watched as her spine and shoulders straightened. Really, she was a marvel. He didn't know many women with such backbone, and though he'd never admit it aloud, he admired her right now.

"Skylar, tell me what's going on."

A brittle laugh scraped past her lips. "Really? Haven't you figured it out already?"

The pieces were slowly falling into place, but he needed the jigsaw finished. "Listen, three women are dead. Three women who bear a striking resemblance to you."

"W—What?" She whirled around, her mouth parted as the blood rushed from her face. *Ah hell*, he'd done it now. Her eyes welled, tears shimmering in those brilliant blue depths. For a moment, he thought she'd lose it, but the woman astounded him once more by pulling herself together at the last moment. "Three? And they look like me?"

Wyatt stiffened. Skylar needed someone here with her, but he needed answers.

"I—I'm sorry," she stammered as she sucked in another cleansing breath. "I'm normally stronger than this."

And he believed it. She'd proven that in spades tonight. With a groan, Wyatt realized he'd pushed her past her breaking point. The woman needed protection, not further harassment. Stuffing his discomfort down deep, he strode across the kitchen and looped his arm around her shoulders. At the sound of a soft hiccup, he drew her into his chest and let her cry it out. Whatever was happening here, it went beyond murder—Wyatt felt it in his bones.

Once her tears were spent, she pushed away from him and wiped the evidence from her cheeks with the heels of her hands. "Did you find where that smell is coming from?"

*Ah, shit.* After her meltdown, the last thing he wanted was to discuss the scene he'd found upstairs. "I did."

She turned shimmering eyes up to him, and his stomach twisted. "And?"

"And don't worry about it."

Sky blinked. "Don't worry about it?"

Regardless of the steel hardening her backbone, he couldn't tell her what he'd found. It would break her, and he wouldn't be the one responsible for that. He might be a bastard, but he wasn't a prick. Wyatt ignored her question and instead fished his cell out of his jeans pocket. The most important thing was getting Skylar somewhere safe. And that meant calling in a few of his pack as a guard detail. Then he needed to phone the sheriff, because if he wasn't mistaken, Skylar's bedroom was the murder scene of the third victim.

"I see you have a bag already?"

Glazed eyes dropped down to the pack at her feet. "I came in here to get it, and when I turned around, he was standing in the doorway."

"You sure it was him?"

Sky shivered against him, a fine tremor that ran from his chest down to his hip. "Yes. I know his scent. I would know it anywhere."

"But you don't know who he is?"

She shook her head, her blonde hair brushing against his skin.

"All right—well, it's something. An identifiable feature. Perhaps there's something to his aroma that we can use to track him."

Unfortunately, thanks to the wind, the man's scent wouldn't lead them beyond the stoop. They'd have to rely on good old-fashioned clues to find the bastard.

"There's someone I think you should speak with," he finally told her.

She tipped her head back, her all-too innocent eyes sucker punching him. "Who?"

"Sheriff Shane Colton."

She blinked, then wiped the few stray tears from her cheeks. "How do you know Shane?"

Wyatt frowned. "How do *you* know Shane?"

"He's been handling my case for the past year. We've become friends." Sky gave a watery chuckle.

Her case? What the hell had this woman gotten herself into?

She reached for her cordless phone. After a few long seconds, she shook her head, picked up the handheld, and dialed. Seemed Sheriff Shane was the first on her speed dial. Wyatt swallowed that particular bit of poison with a grimace. Why should he care what the sheriff meant to her?

*"Oh, my God, Skylar! Where have you been? I've been calling you for the past hour."* Shane's voice came clear through the phone. Wyatt made no attempt to give her any privacy.

"I'm sorry," she whispered. "Shane...he was here. I—I was in the kitchen, and—"

*"I'm already on my way. You were supposed to wait for the patrol car at the airport! They called and told me they couldn't find you."*

"I know. I'm sorry. I saw a cab and thought it'd be all right."

Wyatt's mouth crooked at the sound of Shane cursing.

*"Don't move, all right? I won't be long. There's something we need to discuss."*

He had to give it to her, she held herself together. Shoulders square, she lifted her head and murmured an agreement into the phone.

*"Lock the doors until I get there, all right? Don't ask why. Just do it."*

"It's all right," Sky murmured. "I'm not alone."

"*What do you mean you're not alone? Who's there with you?*"

"His name is Wyatt. He's—"

"*I know who he is. All right. If he's there with you, you're safe. Be patient. I'll be there soon. Can I bring you anything?*"

She sniffled. "Just you."

Shane's chuckle rankled Wyatt. There was no reason for him to feel jealous. It was clear that she and the sheriff had a relationship, and hell, he'd only met her tonight. But that didn't stop the green-eyed monster from pointing and laughing at him.

"*All right, hun. Sit tight.*"

She hung up the phone and turned back to Wyatt, the phone clutched to her chest. "He's on his way."

"So I heard."

"You two know each other?"

Wyatt's head dipped in a slow nod. "I've been helping him on this case."

Her eyes creased. "You mean, the d—deaths?"

He nodded once more.

For the first time since she'd sacked him, she looked up at him with brutal honesty. "I should thank you. Tonight is the first time he's gone this far. If you hadn't been here..." She shivered, a far-off haze dulling her eyes.

The sheer defeat in her words made him want to kill someone. Namely the prick who was the cause of all this. Then Skylar's words punched through him. "Wait, what are you talking about, gone this far?"

Mouth a grim line, she turned and stooped over the

sink, her pack slipping down to her elbow. In that moment, Wyatt realized the full extent of all this.

Sky wasn't only his next intended victim. She was his obsession.

*Time to call in the cavalry.*

---

So close.

So *fucking* close!

His fingers curled into a fist and he pounded it against the wooden floor of the tree fort he'd taken refuge in. The feeble deck shuddered, the planks creaking as they strained to support his weight.

He'd frightened her.

The sharp, blood-curdling scream had startled him more than her. He'd lifted his hands, hoped to placate her, but then he'd heard the alpha rush down the stairs, as much a brute as ever.

He hadn't meant to frighten her, hadn't intended on approaching her. After tonight's chase, he'd thought it best to give her space. But her scent had been far too tempting to ignore. He only wanted to show her how much he loved her. He should have known that she was terrified. Should have slowed down, whispered her name. Should have taken caution, shown discretion. Should have *known* that bastard was in the park and in the house with her tonight. Should have, should have, should have... he raked his fingers over his scalp and pulled on his hair. What he wanted was to scream, to let loose the rage festering within. Every time he got close, she slipped farther away. *So fucking close!*

All he'd wanted was to touch her. Was that so terrible? She was his mate, and all he wanted was to *touch* her.

Anger blazed through his gut, and he pounded his fist a second time, uncaring when the floor teetered.

Next time, he'd take the appropriate steps to prepare her. Rushing into her kitchen in the middle of a windy night hadn't been wise. So much had gone wrong tonight. But he had her phone now. He had full access to her schedule. So he'd leave notes, flowers, candy...anything it took.

The sound of his cell ringing deep in his pocket renewed his sanity. While reaching for it, he pushed his wolf down deep and reminded himself to remain patient —a sentiment he anxiously repeated. The beast prowled the darkest recesses of his mind, slathering for a chance to mate with her. *Soon*, he promised his wolf. Then, it would be the two of them. And nothing would stop him from having his way with her.

*Soon.*

***

Skylar listened half-heartedly as Wyatt phoned in backup. From the muted conversation, it seemed he'd invited his three best men to join the party. Then he'd phoned Shane back, and they'd had a deep discussion that she hadn't been privy to. Deep down, though, she was grateful Wyatt was here, even if he had turned her into a blubbering mess. Her jaw tightened as she stared out the window onto the dark street beyond. She couldn't believe she'd wept in front of him. No, she hadn't simply wept. She'd gone off the reservation and full on ugly-cried. The snively, running nose, blubbering sort of crying, right in front of the alpha of the local pack.

She hadn't lost her cool like that in front of anyone since she was a teenager. After that pitiful event, she'd sworn to herself that no one would ever catch her in such a weak state again. She'd held true to that oath too. Until tonight.

*Ugh.* She bowed her head toward the sink until the embarrassed flush left her cheeks.

She'd believed she could handle this. But every time she thought of that skeevy pervert, he proved her wrong.

Wyatt ended his call with a terse farewell and then turned to lean against the counter next to her. Millimeters away...her stomach warmed with the thought, but touching him was a giant hell no. Everything about him screamed *back off*, from his crossed arms to his ever-so-personable attitude. Was the man physically incapable of smiling?

Not that she minded. The one grin he'd flashed her had nearly been her undoing. And that was *so* not all right.

He shot her a narrowed glance, his mouth pursed. "My wolves were nearby in the city, so we haven't much time before they arrive. In the meantime, why don't you break this down for me? From the beginning, if you don't mind."

"I do mind, actually," she mumbled. "It isn't exactly pleasant conversation."

He stiffened, drawing Sky's gaze to the beautiful tapestry of tattoos that adorned his sculpted chest and muscled arms. Thick swirls inked his flesh in an intricate wolf design that she wanted to trace with the tips of her fingers.

"Like what you see?" he growled.

She wrenched her gaze back up to his, and her heart gave a solid kick when she found him staring down at her. And *goodness*, the man had perfected his stare. Clearing her throat, she stepped back and toed the ground. "Am I not allowed to admire your tattoos?"

"As much as I enjoy being drooled on by an attractive woman, there are more important matters to handle."

Sky's jaw dropped. "Go stuff your ego. I wasn't drooling. Anyone would think they're beautiful."

"Beautiful?" He snorted, offended. "My tattoos are *not* beautiful."

"Well, I think they are. What would you call them?"

He shrugged and regressed back to his stony exterior. "Intimidating and manly."

Of course. With a heavy sigh, Sky pushed away from the counter and strayed toward the middle of the kitchen. Every step only served to remind her that something terrible had happened in her house. While she wanted nothing more than to forget it, the thick stench of death clouded the air. She couldn't let that stop her, though.

A strong hand gripped her arm. "Where are you going?"

Her gaze dropped to the long, tanned fingers that

rested against her arm. The man positively dwarfed her, a feeling she didn't much appreciate when trying to show him that she could handle herself. "To get something to wear," she said, gesturing toward the stairs. "I'd rather not look like this when your wolves arrive. Might give them the wrong idea."

Wyatt's steady gaze studied her length. She told herself to ignore the quick flicker of heat that melted his stony expression. Male werewolves were slaves to their baser instincts, something she'd learned at a young age. They were little more than modern-day cavemen. Hell, the man could hate the woman, but the moment his wolf spotted a decent pair of legs, he was howling at the moon like a randy mutt. So, why then, did her pulse suddenly decide to take off?

"You have a bag right here." Was it her imagination, or did he sound like he'd swallowed a mouthful of gravel?

She glanced down at the rucksack and grimaced. While it was true that she'd packed it with the intent of running, she'd chosen clothes she rarely wore. What she wanted was the comfy hoodie her father had given her as a graduation gift and her baggy pajama pants. She wanted clothes that swallowed her whole.

It was now or never. She refused to let her unfriendly neighborhood stalker steal something else from her. That sweater was her favorite; she refused to leave it behind. Squaring her shoulders, she marched forward. "I'll be right back. It won't take a second to run upstairs—"

"No."

And *there* it was. That word again—one she was starting to loathe. "Excuse me?"

Wyatt stooped over and yanked open her bag. Before she could blink, he stuffed his hands within and started tearing out her personal possessions. "Here." He shoved a wad of clothing into her arms. "Wear these."

Her ears still buzzed from the word *no*. Growling under her breath, she dropped the clothes to the floor and darted up the stairs. How he managed to turn everything into a pissing contest was beyond her.

She felt him behind her, felt the weight of his gaze burning through her shoulder.

"Sky, I said—"

A litany of curses fell from her lips, and mid-step, she pivoted and glared down on him. For the first time since they'd met that night, she had the height advantage. Lording it over him, she pressed forward until the two were near touching. "I'll remind you again that you are not my alpha."

Deep and dark, his growl lifted the hairs on the back of her neck.

"And that this is my house, Wyatt." The height advantage bolstered her courage. She leaned forward and tapped him on the nose, swallowing at the sudden flash of desire in his eyes. "You can come with me if you want, but—"

She never got the rest of the invitation out. The last thing she'd expected was for the man to pin her against the wall and knock her shoes off with a soul-searing kiss.

Stunned, Sky's mouth fell open, and Wyatt took full advantage. She sucked in a breath the moment his tongue caressed hers, the hard press of his lips curling her toes. Magic slammed into her as he plundered her mouth.

*Goodness*, the man could kiss. Strong arms curved around her waist and braced her against the wall as he deepened the angle.

*Mate...*her wolf gave a long, earthy howl, pacing anxiously as the magic swelled between them. Sky melted into his embrace, stricken by the strength of the connection between them. No matter how much she loathed the man, her wolf had an entirely different opinion.

Wyatt broke from the kiss and stared down at her, annoyance tapering his gaze as he snarled, "Shit."

*Shit, indeed.*

Growling, he swept down and kissed her again. In that instant, Sky knew she was done for.

# 6

W yatt hadn't a clue what he was doing. One moment, the damned she-wolf had been lecturing him and tapping him on the nose like he was nothing more than a troublesome pup, and the next, he had her plastered against the wall. Except, the moment their lips touched, he *knew*. His wolf rejoiced, howling at the proverbial moon that he'd finally found his mate.

He groaned and shifted his weight against her, his left hand sweeping down her curved length to grasp her bare thigh. *Hello*...smooth and hot and tantalizing. He guided it above his hip, as he'd imagined doing on his bike tonight, and ground himself against her, his eyes crossing when she grazed against the hard ridge in his jeans.

The T-shirt had to go. As lovely as the dark color was against her tanned skin, he wanted nothing between them. His hand delved beneath the hem of the shirt, his fingers brushing against the soft arc of her breast. She purred against his mouth, a sound that grew obnoxiously loud until Wyatt realized it wasn't her. With a frustrated grunt, he nipped her bottom lip and ran his thumb over her enticingly taut nipple before he pushed himself away. *Untimeliest of timings*...he sighed and raked a hand through his hair. Why didn't it surprise him that their backup had arrived now of all times?

Sky stood silently by. Nimble fingers leapt to her mouth and she traced the supple curve of the rosy lip he'd caught between his teeth. Impassioned eyes watched him as he backed into the far wall, her other hand clutching at the neck of the T-shirt. Seemed she wasn't the only one startled by the situation. Any other day and he would have rolled her six ways from Sunday, regardless of how much she aggravated him. But with the return of his senses came the understanding that this could not happen again. He didn't want a mate, and from the horrified look on her face, she didn't either. He had no intentions of getting involved with a woman whose life had been hijacked by some disturbed stalker.

Wyatt cleared his throat and adjusted his pants before starting down the stairs. "They're here."

Still, she didn't speak.

He stole one final glance, his heart—and a more southern appendage—throbbing at the sight of her flushed cheeks and well-kissed mouth. He mentally kicked himself and recited all the reasons he couldn't climb the stairs and have his way with her. Not only was there a crime scene one level up—and nothing said sexy like a bloody mattress—but their wolves wouldn't allow them to fuck without fulfilling the mating call. He'd have to plunge more than his dick into her, and like hell he'd sink his fangs into a woman he'd only just met. "Downstairs, now."

Her lashes fluttered, but for once, she held her sinful tongue. Unnerving. Had he known the mating call was all it would take to silence her, he might have kissed her earlier.

Refusing to dwell further on her taciturn behaviour, he stalked down the stairs and grabbed the pile of discarded clothing. "Put these on before they come inside."

The fiery tang of anger drifted down the stairwell. Clearly, she loathed it when he ordered her around, but he hadn't the time for a more diplomatic approach. His wolves were here, and in a few minutes, they would be storming the castle, so to speak. And while his head screamed that he couldn't touch her again, his dick ached for her. He'd be damned before he allowed any of his wolves to catch his mate standing around half-naked. His fingers twitched. Not mate, *Sky*.

At the foot of the stairs, he listened as she yanked on a sweater and zipped up a pair of jeans. Relieved, he stepped through the kitchen and held open the door.

"Welcome to the murder house," he muttered to his men as they crossed the threshold.

"And people say you never take me anywhere nice," Harley teased as he stepped inside, his fingers plugging his nose.

Wyatt greeted the other two with quick pats on the back, then turned to introduce Sky. The woman brushed by the four of them with hardly a glance. Anger and frustration perfumed the tainted air, and, as one, his boys lifted their brows.

"Skylar, this is Bale, my beta. And those two fools over there with their fingers up their noses are Axel and Harley."

She came to a stop at the sink and gave a delicate snort. "Those aren't their real names."

Harley extricated his fingers and threw her a wide grin. "No, ma'am." With her back to them, Harley's sickeningly sweet grin morphed into a smirk before he elbowed Axel and gestured toward Sky's backside. Wyatt had seen that look grace the man's face before—it was one Harley sported before he turned on the charm.

A curse darkened Wyatt's lips before he could catch himself. Together, his wolves turned toward him, but it was Harley whose brow arched. The memory of Sky's mouth still lingered on his—he sure as shit wasn't going to stand by and watch another wolf eye-hump her.

Why did she have to look so adorable, anyway? The hoodie he'd thrown her way was much too large. The UCLA sweater swam on her lithe form, but those jeans... he swallowed. The blasted things looked painted on, and hell if his palms weren't itching for another handful.

"So, what's up, boss?" Axel waggled his eyebrows, his Cajun accent mangling the common phrase. "Sounds like you've had an interesting night so far."

*Interesting.* That was one way of putting it. A simple evening ride had turned into a nightmare, in more than one way. The most distressing of which was the discovery of his supposed headstrong mate.

Grunting, Wyatt reached down and snatched up

Sky's small knapsack. He jerked his head toward the bikes. "Mount up. She comes with us. We ride hard. I want no mistakes. We aren't followed, hear me? And if we are, take care of it."

"W—What?" Sky whirled around, her blue eyes like ice. "No, absolutely not. I'm not going anywhere with you. I don't know you! Plus, Shane's on his way."

Wyatt leaned toward her. "I'm not arguing this with you. Shane will be busy processing the scene upstairs for a few hours. You're coming with us, and I don't want to hear anything more about it."

The tension in the room ramped up. Axel and Harley shared a shocked glance. Honestly, Wyatt had expected such a response. The woman seemed incapable of accepting help. From an alpha's point of view, it made sense to show no weakness. But regardless of how dominant she played, she wasn't an alpha.

Sky's face mottled with frustration. "I never asked for your help!"

"Most people would say *thank you*."

"Thank you, but *no* thank you."

Wyatt's jaw ticked. "For crying out loud, Sky. Stop acting childish."

Harley sucked in a sharp breath.

"Go hump a leg," she growled. "You don't control my life. You don't get to decide what I do! Not to mention that I have a *job*, one that expects me across the country by tomorrow afternoon."

"Ya, ya, we get it. You're a strong, independent woman. Hurray. But look at this logically, darling. Whoever this guy is, he isn't going to stop until he finds you. And when he does, you're going to need the help. Going at this alone is stupid. So, call your boss and tell him that, as of this moment, you're on vacation."

"Vacation!" she sputtered. "You haven't the first clue what my job entails. I can't just go on vacation!"

"Sure you can. Everyone is entitled to a vacation. You tell him, or I will."

She let out a humorless laugh, her eyes blazing. "Try it!"

"Oh, for the love of Christ, woman!" He wanted to punch something. What the hell was it with her? Why did she need to make things so difficult? Couldn't she graciously accept his help?

"Uh, guys?" Axel stepped between them with his hands held up. "As riveting as this is, I think everyone should take a deep breath and calm down."

Wyatt's head snapped toward his fourth-in-command. "Excuse me?"

Axel cringed backward at the sound of Wyatt's menacing voice. "Forgive me, Alpha. I don't know exactly what's going on between you two, but my guess is that we can't stand here arguing all night."

Wyatt sucked in a deep breath and turned back to Sky. Axel was right, but that didn't mean he had to like it. "I'm not going to go through this with you again. When I said you were coming with us, I wasn't asking."

"Why are you doing this?" she asked in a hushed whisper, low enough that he hoped the others couldn't hear.

He gritted his teeth. "It's my job to protect you. To

protect *any* wolf that's in trouble. I may not be the nicest guy in the world, but I take my responsibilities seriously."

With her anger spent, the color drained from her cheeks until she stood ashen faced before him. Her expression had him questioning his response. Had he said something wrong? Was her cooperation such a difficult thing to promise?

"Seems I don't have a choice."

Wyatt cursed. "Why do I feel like I kicked a puppy?"

She offered a wan smile that punched him in the heart, and then she slipped out from under him and went to fetch her bag. "There are some things I would like from my room. But your illustrious leader over there won't let me upstairs. Would someone be willing to grab some things for me?"

His jaw tightened. Every inch of her screamed meek and vulnerable. And he hated it. What happened to the spitfire that had head butted him? "I'll go." Like hell he was going to let anyone else paw through her belongings.

She nodded and listed off a few belongings before snatching up the phone and dialing her boss' number.

"Stay vigilant," he reminded his wolves before he trudged up the stairs.

## 7

————————

Sky all but flew off the bike the moment Wyatt geared down. Pulse all a-flutter, she stalked clear across the garage and analyzed her surroundings. Nothing spectacular, just a man parking his motorcycle in his uncluttered shop. Everything seemed to have its place. Everything except her. She *so* didn't belong here, didn't belong on any pack turf. Her former alpha had made the terms rather clear when he'd exiled her nearly six years ago.

"Got a thing for wood?"

She sucked in a sharp breath and whirled around, loose strands of hair snaking around her neck. "Excuse me?"

He rose from his bike, his denim-clad legs straddling the chopper. Sky's mouth dried, her heart giving a kick when her traitorous mind replayed the scene from her house. With a deep breath, she forced the image away. The last thing she needed to think about right now was that smoldering kiss that would have scorched her panties, had she been wearing any.

Wyatt removed his helmet, the movement distracting her from such thoughts. He jerked his chin toward the shelving. "You've been staring at those shelves since we pulled in."

She turned back to the shelves in question. Truthfully, she had barely noticed them in her need to escape his overwhelming presence. An eternity had passed since he'd ordered her to mount the bike behind him—and hell, if her cheeks hadn't burned when he'd uttered that word. The long ride had been torturous, feeling his every muscle shift beneath her as he flawlessly controlled his motorcycle, not to mention the heat his body put off. The worst had been the sharp turns that had forced her to clutch at him. Her damned palm still burned from the feel of his hard chest beneath it. And just like that, the lightbulb flicked on above her head. The bastard had *purposely* taken the turns hard, forcing her to scramble and grab for him so as not to fall off the bike.

Her mouth twisted. Of course he had.

"Listen, darling, now that we have a minute alone, we need to talk about what happened back there."

She blinked, and, with a harsh breath, pushed her bangs back from her face. She hated this. How did he look so fine when she felt as though she'd been raked over coals? "Believe me, there's *nothing* to discuss. The next time you feel the need to shove your tongue down my throat, don't."

Wyatt pushed away from his bike, his face

74

inscrutable as he studied her. "You saying you didn't enjoy it?"

Her cheeks flushed. *For crying out loud*, of course he had to ask *that*. "No one enjoys being slobbered on."

A look of true insult crossed his face. "Sweetheart, I've never slobbered on a woman in my entire life."

"Men," she said with a disgusted scoff.

"Like women are any better," he muttered. "But that's not what I was talking about."

"I don't want to talk about *that* either, all right? I'm not looking for a mate. So, let's forget it." Her wolf snarled in her head.

"I'm not exactly jumping up and down for joy either, darling."

"Don't call me that." Frustrated, she ripped the elastic out of her hair and shook out her platinum mane.

The darkness in his eyes abated for a moment as he watched her sweep it back once more and secure it into a quick knot. "As much as I enjoy the sexy librarian fantasy you've got going for you right now, I much prefer your hair down. Don't tie it back on my account."

She froze with her fingers at the back of her neck. With a withering glare, she yanked it back tighter. "I don't recall asking your opinion."

"Don't recall caring," Wyatt shot back before he ascended the stairs. "You coming or what?"

After a long ten hours on the plane, not to mention the *lovely* adventure at her house, then the time it'd taken to arrive here, she was about ready to drop. At this point, all she longed for was somewhere to rest her head, even if that place was a hard floor.

"Boss, glad to see you two made it one piece." Axel sidled up to them, his gaze flicking between them. "Everything all right?"

Sky bit her tongue. She had to remember that she was on his turf now. Speaking out of turn could earn her a one-way ticket to death row. And no matter how independent she'd grown in the past years, she knew well enough to avoid that.

"Right as rain," Wyatt assured him before striding through the house.

Axel and Sky shared a hesitant glance. Unsure whether or not to follow, Sky eased away from the wall and drifted forward. Her eyes roamed the expansive interior. *Holy hell*, the last thing she'd expected was a bloody mansion. Mouth agape, she circled the first room she stumbled upon. From the look of the large television perched before the couch, she guessed it to be the living room.

At first glance, this house seemed ill-fitted to Wyatt. Everything about him screamed hard-ass, but this house... it appeared well-cared for. As though it possessed a woman's touch. Delicate wall hangings and a lovely carpet that ran the length of the floor welcomed her. The furniture was a touch worn but both the supple couch and matching armchair possessed an air of comfort. Between them sat a cooler teeming with beer, and to the left was the start of what appeared to be a beer can fortress, towers included. The entire house was a mess of contrasts, one she couldn't wrap her head around; yet, instantly, she knew she liked it. There was a warm aura to the place, quite unlike hers, thanks to her stalker.

76

She turned, her gaze landing upon a group of three men that hovered around a prized pool table made of lush green felt and cherry mahogany wood. She watched as the cue ball banked off the side of the table, then darted toward the small cluster of gleaming billiard balls. And when a striped ball rebounded into the nearest pocket, two of the men roared their enjoyment and high-fived one another. She hadn't seen such camaraderie in ages, even among the humans. With a job like hers—public advocacy for werewolves—the humans knew she wasn't one of them. It had made for some lonely Saturday nights. Though she loathed the circumstances in which Shane had entered her life, she at least appreciated the friend. And a true friend he was.

"Welcome to our little abode," Axel murmured in his delightful accent.

She did another turnabout, noting the larger group that lingered near a dart board. The chalkboard next to them was covered with cramped scribbles, but at first count, the side with Wyatt's name appeared to be in the lead.

"Alpha!" a boisterous voice boomed through the house.

She stumbled into Axel when yet another giant-sized man rushed by her. What the hell was Wyatt feeding them? Even the women she spotted were immense.

"Easy, *chère*," Axel chuckled. "Wouldn't do for you to get run over, now would it?"

"What is this place?" She watched, astounded, as two smaller-framed females raced to the couch, breathlessly laughing as they tussled over the one red console controller.

"Home," Axel said with a half-shrug. "We don't all live here. The house can lodge ten of us at any time. There are currently eight of us—nine if you include the alpha—who live here permanently. The rest have their own lodgings spread throughout the community." Axel stepped forward with her bag in hand. "Come, Sky. Let's get you settled into a room."

Now *that* she could support.

"One hour," Wyatt called as he strode toward the dart board.

"*Oui, mon ami.*"

Sky ignored Wyatt's vague words until she and Axel were upstairs and out of sight. Once he pointed her toward the only remaining empty room, she turned and inquired about the stated time limit with an arched brow.

"Your police friend will be here by then," Axel informed her as he lowered her bag down onto the bed then set about snapping the curtains shut. "To keep out prying eyes," he said when he caught her arched brow.

Her blood turned to ice, reminding her that her life had taken yet another skewed turn to Shittyville.

A firm hand settled on her shoulder as gentle fingers guided her chin up. "You are strong, *chère*. You'll get through this. But we're here to protect you as well."

"From Wyatt too?" Her voice warbled, but her mouth curved as she delivered the weak joke. Her entire life she'd prayed that she'd never come across her so-called destined mate. And now that she'd met him, she remembered why.

Axel joined in with a low chuckle of his own. "Nah, you're screwed there."

"Is he always such a dick?"

A strange glint appeared in Axel's dark brown eyes. "He's in a rough mood tonight. Things will seem better tomorrow."

She blew out a heavy breath and nodded. "One hour, right?"

"Fear not," he chuckled. "Someone will fetch you if your sheriff arrives before you're ready."

"Thanks." She closed the door behind his retreating figure and set to unpacking.

Her attention drifted toward the bed. A plush eyelet quilt beckoned. She drifted closer and ran her hand over the soft material. An hour wasn't much time, but at this point, she'd take anything. A moment later, she curled atop the bedspread and fell asleep with her head cradled between two plump pillows.

**8**

———

"Where's the girl?"

Wyatt's head rose at the sound of Bale's voice. His beta paced into the room and threw himself down into the nearest chair, leg hooked over the armrest. The man looked the picture of ease and grace, which only annoyed Wyatt further. For the past forty minutes, he'd been scouring the Web for any information regarding the three victims. Shane had warned him that they were keeping it quiet, and from the whole whopping squat he'd found, they'd succeeded.

At one point, he'd considered asking Sky, until he recalled the look of absolute shock when he'd mentioned the three victims. Seemed Shane had a lot to answer for, and he couldn't imagine the sheriff was looking forward to that conversation.

"Earth to Wyatt." Bale waved a hand in front of his face.

"I don't know. She's somewhere," Wyatt muttered.

He shifted in his chair and turned back to the computer, fingers clacking furiously against the keyboard as he ran yet another search.

"Ah, thanks, I gathered that much."

Wyatt cast a tapered glance toward his beta. "Why do you care where she is?"

A low chuckle graced Bale's lips. "Oh, you know, maybe because we're supposed to be protecting her."

"There are a dozen werewolves in this house at any given time. I'm sure she's fine."

"Yo." Bale rapped his knuckles against Wyatt's mahogany desk. "Have you forgotten that there's some sick bastard out there gunning for her? Because I sure haven't."

Wyatt sighed and dropped his head into his hands. Of course he hadn't forgotten—rather, didn't want to think about it. It ate at him that she was in danger. "What do you want, Bale?"

"The girl's on the news. Thought she might want to see, since her life is about to change dramatically."

"What?" Wyatt's head snapped up. "What do you mean she's on the news?"

Bale's mouth quirked. "I mean someone took some not-so-lovely pictures of her house, and they're airing it live right now."

With a mumbled curse, Wyatt snatched his remote off the desk and flicked on the television. He cranked up the volume and leaned forward on his desk, his gut twisting when an image of Sky's house flashed across his screen.

A female reporter's voice kicked in mid-sentence.

"*...the whereabouts of Werewolf Public Advocate Skylar Callahan are currently unknown—*"

Wyatt blinked. *Werewolf public advocate?*

"*Dios mío.*" Bale straightened in his seat and leaned over, elbows perched between his knees. "I knew I recognized her. A man does not forget a woman like her," he murmured, grinning when he caught Wyatt's harsh glare. "Ah, I had wondered..."

"Wondered what, boyo?"

The corner of Bale's mouth twitched. "When I saw the two of you together, snapping at each other like children, I had wondered if maybe—"

"Oh, *hell no*," Wyatt hissed. "That's a thought process you are *not* to encourage." It was bad enough that his wolf craved her; he did *not* need his men introducing such thoughts to the pack.

"Is that so? You mean to tell me that we didn't interrupt anything earlier—"

"Bale!"

"All right," Bale mused as he dropped back into the chair. "So what if she and I..." His brow winged up.

A raw growl scraped past Wyatt's lips.

His beta lifted his hands. "Tell me if she's off-limits, boss."

"She is absolutely, unequivocally off-limits."

Bale ran his hand across his lips. "Because...?"

Wyatt sucked in a sharp breath and whipped the remote control across the room, his jaw setting when it shattered against the wall. "Because I said so. And this topic is closed." He met his beta's stare with one of his own, his lip curled back over his teeth.

"Ah, because that is a sane reaction."

Wyatt's eyes shuttered and he dropped his head into his hands. "Don't push me, Bale."

"Wouldn't dream of it, boss."

His second's sardonic voice rubbed him the wrong way. Massaging the tension out of his temples, he directed a sly glance back to his computer. *Werewolf public advocate*...he'd recognized Sky's name when she'd first given it, but hadn't been able to place exactly where he'd heard it. Now that he knew, he almost wished he didn't. The last thing he wanted was a high-profile mate.

Turning his chair back to his computer, he pulled the keyboard closer and typed in her name. He shouldn't have been surprised to find multiple pages focused on her. Seemed Skylar had established herself among the political and academic crowds. What the hell did a Master's in Sociocultural Evolutionism with a specialization in werewolves entail, anyhow?

Multiple social media sites flashed her image. Hell, she even had her own website. Thumbing through the tabs, he brought up the images of her and his jaw dropped. Was it any wonder she'd attracted a stalker?

The creak of the chair across from him alerted him to Bale's movement, and a moment later, a shadow dropped over him as his beta came for a look.

"Well, damn." Bale released a low whistle. "Looks like our girl has been making quite the name for herself."

Dancing at a presidential ball...no, Sky had already made a name for herself. And *boy howdy*, she looked stunning in a low-backed gold ball gown. Hell, he steered clear of the media, and even he'd seen this photo when it hit the newsstands. How could he have forgotten?

"Look here." Bale tapped the screen. "Escorted by Senator Samuel Cohan."

*Sweet Lord*, the woman had contacts. So what the hell was she doing in Wolffe Peak, Colorado?

The sound of her name drew Wyatt's and Bale's attention away from the computer and back toward the television.

*"Skylar Callahan was last spotted in Washington, D.C. not three days ago, campaigning for werewolf awareness, seen here."*

An image of Skylar flashed across the screen. Wyatt studied her length, noting how they'd hidden her curves beneath well-tailored suits, lending an air of professionalism to her otherwise feminine form. With one ear, he listened to her speech about equality between humans and werewolves. The other guided his attention to the office door, where Skylar had appeared.

It was quite the change, seeing her now in a plain white tank top and low-riding jeans. He much preferred this look compared to the expensive suits. Tank top and jeans, he could accommodate that sort of lifestyle. Ball gowns and fancy parties, not so much.

Her gaze shot across the room to the television, and she winced at the sight of her house lit up with flood lights. Police vehicles and professionals surrounded her home, clearly investigating the scene they'd discovered in her bedroom.

She entered the room with her chin lifted in a show of strength. "So, now you know who I am."

Indeed. Now he knew. Not that it changed a damned thing. Stunning ball gowns, hideous suits, or down-to-earth jeans, he still wanted her. And Wyatt wasn't in the business of denying himself something he wanted. Mate or not.

"Ah, welcome *querida*." Bale rounded the desk and dropped back into the chair. With a rakish grin meant entirely for Wyatt, he hooked his foot around a second chair and pulled it flush against his before patting it lasciviously. "Have a seat."

Snarling, Wyatt planted his foot against the edge of Bale's chair and gave a strong push. He'd meant to shove him across the room, but with the wolf's balance teetering toward the back of the seat, the extra weight sent the chair into a backward spiral. The sight of Bale's wide eyes brought a harsh laugh to Wyatt's lips, but it was nothing compared to the image of his second's arms pin-wheeling moments before he tumbled backward to the floor, his long legs flipping over his head.

A long, drawn-out moan sounded from the floor. Wyatt leaned over his desk with a cocked brow and stared down at his beta. "Lesson learned?"

Bale groaned and rubbed the back of his head. "Quite emphatically." Picking himself up, he righted the chair, then plopped back into it, a sullen expression twisting his face. "And I'm fine, thank you. Your concern is overwhelming."

"Are you bleeding?"

He touched his hand to the back of his head and winced. "No."

"Then shut up."

Sky's dulcet voice piped up from the corner of the room. "Are you seeing double? You hit your head pretty hard. Do you remember your name?"

Bale blinked and then slid a coy smile in her direction. "Ah, *querida*, your concern is touching."

Wyatt kept his eyes on his second, his jaw tight. "He's fine, Sky. Bale, go fetch the others. The sheriff should be here any moment now. Wait downstairs until he arrives. Then bring them all up. I'd like a few moments to speak with Sky. Alone."

She sucked in a sharp breath and glanced his way, her teeth nibbling at the corner of her lip.

Bale gave a terse nod and rose from his seat, the humor wiped clean from his face. He left the room, and Wyatt indicated that Sky should sit.

"I don't know." Her mouth pursed. "What if you decide to push me over?"

He cut her a sharp glance. "Bale's used to it."

She placed her arms on the armrests and eased into the seat. "Your beta is used to being pushed around by you? Good to know."

He cursed and grabbed a pencil from the corner of his desk, idly spinning it between his fingers. "That's not what I meant."

A twinkle of playfulness sparked in her eye. "I know."

Wyatt stared. She was beautiful. There was something open and honest about her. And after all she'd been through today, he admired her ability to keep things light. *Admired*. That was a word he wouldn't have thought himself capable of. There were so few in his life whom he held in high regard. In one night, Sky had wormed her way onto that short list.

He lowered the pencil down onto the desk and faced her with brutal honesty. Keep it business. "When Shane arrives, he and my first three will join us."

Fear whisked across her face, but she merely nodded.

"There are things I need to know. If we're going to stop this bastard, I need *all* the information." He silently applauded himself for maintaining a calm and steady voice. It seemed he could be nice when the situation arose. Not that he'd ever felt the need to do so before tonight.

Her hands shifted into her lap where she clasped them together and gave another terse nod.

"That means we might have to discuss things that are hard for you to talk about."

Another nod. She glanced down into her lap, a stray lock of hair slipping over her shoulder. Her vulnerability punched Wyatt in the gut.

"I'm not going to apologize for having to ask you the hard questions. This is important."

A fourth nod.

"Damn it, say something. Don't just sit there nodding," he growled. All right, so he'd run out of "nice".

"I get it, Wyatt." She cleared her throat and lifted her head. "You don't need to coddle me. I won't break."

"Glad to hear it." He glanced at the door and gestured for his men to enter.

"Ah, *chère*, glad to see you a little more alert." Axel sidled up next to her and squeezed her shoulder before taking up his usual post against the far left wall.

Harley entered next, a giant grin tugging on his mouth as Bale followed behind him. The moment Wyatt's gaze met Bale's, he groaned. Whatever had transpired between his men downstairs, Bale and Harley looked a touch too smug for his liking.

"Sky!"

Her head snapped up, and she rose from the chair. "Shane!"

The two embraced. Snarling, Wyatt returned to his computer with the hope of striking that particular image from his memory. His wolf demanded blood, fangs gnashing at the sight of another man touching his mate. *Get it together, boyo.*

"One big happy family, eh?" Bale laughed as he strode into the room.

"Enough. Sit." Wyatt gestured toward the empty seats. He sure as hell wasn't going to be the only one sitting. Normally, he was content in his strength, but everything about tonight had him on edge.

A pile of folders rested in Shane's lap. At first glance, Wyatt counted four. Three were gray, the fourth a pale blue. Seemed the local enforcement color-coded the offenses.

"Sky, the floor is yours."

Her pained cornflower eyes knocked the breath out of him. It took effort, but Wyatt softened his gaze and offered a small grin.

Sky blanched at the sight of it. Clearing his throat, Wyatt swallowed the smile. He'd never admit it aloud, but he knew the effect of his scars, so rather than submit her to them, he turned and took up Axel's previous post.

"It's all right," Shane whispered. "Start from the beginning. Pretend you're talking to me."

She nodded, her messy ponytail bobbing at the back of her head. "It started after my mother's funeral a little over a year ago." Her tenuous hold on the armrests broke, and she brought her hands together in her lap, once more.

"Her mother was a member of the Pacific Coast Pack," Shane informed them.

She nodded, her gaze burning a hole through the floor. "The official cause of her death is still unknown. And right now, unimportant."

"*Chère...*"

She shook her head. "I don't say that for your sympathy. My mother and I were not on speaking terms. I hadn't seen her in over ten years."

Wyatt shifted against the wall. He hadn't had a chance to go through her personal file, and he had warned her he would ask questions. "Weren't you part of the same pack?" It was impossible for two pack members to go so long without speaking.

She flicked a glance his way. "When I left my pack at seventeen to attend university, my mother refused to speak with me. She felt I had turned my back on them all. I'll spare you the tiresome details, but eventually, my pack exiled me."

Wyatt shook his head. "Can't gloss over that, darling."

She tensed, eyes blazing. "I'm *not* your darling, and it isn't important," she said. "My alpha thought my place was with the pack. I was expected to mate, and when I refused to pick someone, he claimed I didn't have the pack's best interest at heart. I was told under no uncertain terms that I was no longer a member. It doesn't matter. I've been managing fine on my own."

"Really." Wyatt's sardonic tone drew the attention of the group back to him. "Doesn't seem that way to me. You know, stalker and all that."

"Listen, you pompous—"

Bale cleared his throat. "All right. So you mentioned your mother's funeral."

She threw Wyatt another glare. "After the funeral, I returned home and buried myself in my work. I'd been making such progress with Congress, and—" She shook her head. "That's not important either. A few days after the funeral, the phone calls started." Her voice wavered, and she pressed her hands to her cheeks as though to will away unseen tears. "I didn't think anything of them at first. I thought it was someone from my old pack having a laugh at my expense. It started off as nothing more than silence, but then..."

"Then?"

Pain flickered across her face, and Sky turned away. "At first there was only heavy breathing, but then..." A shiver rippled down her spine.

Wyatt tensed. This didn't sound right, at all. "Sky?"

"There's one particular call I'll never forget." She cleared her throat and lifted her head, her gaze lost beyond the window. "It started with panting. I panicked and demanded to know who it was. I—I thought it was someone from my pack. The harassing phone calls hadn't started until I returned from the funeral, so it had to have been one of them, right?"

Logically, it made sense. Wyatt made a note to check out the alpha and arrange a conversation.

"And then I heard a soft grunt and a long exhale. I—I heard shuffling in the background. And then..." Her breath hitched. "His moans still haunt my nightmares. I should have hung up the phone, but I was stunned. I sat there, frozen, and listened."

"Are you saying he...?"

She broke, her head dropping forward. "I didn't want to believe it at first. But then he called again. And again. And every time it was the same."

Wyatt's hands fisted at his sides. What kind of a sick bastard masturbated over the phone? *Oh, right, the kind who carves out little girls' eyes.* And didn't that thought make him all warm and tingly inside? And murderous. Very, very murderous.

"I did everything I could think of. I reported the phone calls to the police. Shane suggested I record the calls for evidence, and I did, but nothing useable ever came from them. He attempted to track the calls, but again, nothing."

"Burner phone," Harley piped up.

Sky turned around. "A what?"

"Prepaid cell phones," Wyatt grumbled. "Untraceable unless a credit card is attached to them. Of course, if you're using a burner phone, you wouldn't attach your credit card to it."

Her gaze connected with his, free of contempt this time. "How do you know that?"

He shrugged. "Go on."

"After that, I did the only thing I could think of. I changed my phone number."

"Did the calls stop?"

"For a while," she admitted. "I thought I was safe."

"But?"

"But then the letters started."

Harley pushed off the wall and strode across the room as though he needed to pace in order to think. "What letters?" Wyatt watched as the former FBI agent within rose to the surface. The man all but vibrated with excitement, as though he missed the game.

"Small notes," she whispered. She held Wyatt's gaze, and though he wasn't the best at offering comfort, he nodded and forced another small smile. "He would slip them under my door. It got to the point where I couldn't sleep at night, terrified he would break in. The police started doing hourly patrols. They suggested I install a security system, and I did. It even included a camera, but somehow he knew about it. All the tapes they collected, they never caught a glimpse of his face. The only thing I knew was that he was a werewolf. I could smell it on the letters."

"These letters..." Wyatt turned the conversation back to them. "What did they say?"

A furious blush painted her cheeks. "I—I'd rather not repeat them. If you need to read them, Shane has them. I turned them over to him, and his people came and did a sweep of my house. They fingerprinted the door, the stoop, the letters...nothing. They never found a single piece of DNA." She choked on her next sentence and dropped her head, severing the connection between them. "Until they found his semen on my windowsill."

Unadulterated rage swept through Wyatt. *Murder, yup, with a side of castration.*

"They ran his DNA, but it didn't generate a hit, so there wasn't much more the police could do. At first, Shane assigned a patrol to drive by hourly. But that only lasted so long. He learned their schedule and would come between their shifts. So Shane started staying with me."

Wyatt snarled. "*With* you, as in—"

"As in on my couch, you ass!" she hissed.

The sheriff's tight gaze flicked to Wyatt, his brow lifted as though confused by the purpose of such an inane question. Not that Wyatt had a logical reason beyond the personal satisfaction of learning they weren't sleeping together.

"Eventually, we decided it would be best if I moved, so I did. I bought an unlisted two-bedroom house, and Shane moved in permanently."

He shivered with rage. Well, wasn't that a jolly piece of news. The friggin' sheriff *lived* with Skylar. He'd noticed the man's scent there tonight, but he'd thought it nothing more than visits. "Good to know the local law enforcement takes such a personal interest in their cases."

Shane blinked. "Excuse me?"

Sky lurched from the chair and bore down on him. "Listen, buddy. You said you would ask questions, and I agreed, but leave Shane out of it, all right?"

Wyatt's gaze flicked down to the finger she'd jabbed into his chest, above his crossed arms. For a moment, he was tempted to drag her into his chest and show her how badly he wanted to leave Shane out of it. His good sense returned, and, instead, he curled a lip and warned her in a dark voice, "Step back, Sky."

"No! You've been nothing but a condescending asshole. And I'm sick of it. You can insult me all you want, but Shane has been nothing but supportive. It was his idea for me to move, and once I did, I'll have you know the letters and calls all but stopped."

Now wasn't that an important bit of information. Wyatt's gaze slid to the sheriff, whose cheeks still burned from Wyatt's implication.

Bale's hands curved over Sky's shoulders and guided her back. "Calm yourself, *querida*."

"I'm calm," she bit out with a final growl before returning to her seat. "I lived in peace for a few months." She shot each of them a glance. "And that's all."

"Until tonight," Wyatt stated. "Except that isn't all. Is it, Sheriff?"

Shane fiddled with the folders in his hands and finally shook his head. "I'm sorry, Sky. I should have told you sooner, but I didn't want to frighten you more than you already were."

She frowned.

"Get on with it," Wyatt growled impatiently.

The sooner this was out in the open, the sooner they could find this bastard and ram his head onto a pike.

## 9
---

"I shouldn't be discussing an ongoing case such as this," Shane stated as he pushed up from his seat with a deep sigh. "But Sky's safety is more important."

"And if you're caught?" Wyatt rumbled from across the room.

"Well, the position of sheriff is electoral, so I assume come next election, I wouldn't win." His comforting brown gaze slid to hers. "But I think this case requires special care."

"I bet," Wyatt muttered.

Lips set in a grim line, Shane strode across the room and pointed to a whiteboard. "May I?"

No one spoke, which Shane took as an affirmation, and he wiped clean the board. "At this point, we have three victims."

Sky shuddered. *Victims*, such a visceral word.

The dry erase marker squeaked against the board as Shane wrote out three names: *Barbara Jackson, Erica*

*Marsters*, and *Jody Anne Davidson*. Next came their pictures. Sky sucked in a sharp breath, her heart palpitating at the sight of the three young ladies. Wyatt had mentioned that they resembled her, but never in her wildest dreams...

"Sky?"

It wasn't until Bale whispered her name that she realized she had risen from her chair and approached the board. Her fingers hovered above the last picture.

"Blonde hair, blue eyes," she repeated Wyatt's comment from earlier in the night.

But it went beyond that. All three—four, if she included herself—bore the same facial structure and skin tone. It was downright eerie to see so much of herself reflected on a foreign eight-and-half-inch glossy photo.

"Barbara Jackson was found two months ago, at the bottom of Humming Creek." Shane brushed against Sky's shoulder and drew the woman's picture down. She stood in a crowd, embraced by two other women, all with bright smiles. "Her case was treated as an isolated event. Her wounds were consistent with a long fall. The condition of her, ah..." Shane cleared his throat, "eyes was assumed to be a result of wildlife. It wouldn't have been the first time a carrion bird got to a body before us."

"Eyes." Sky glanced over her shoulder, her gaze skipping from Shane to Wyatt. She shivered at the sight of him, inclined against the wall with his burly arms crossed over his chest, and turned back to Shane. Shane was safer. Shane was docile and comforting. Wyatt scared the hell out of her. "What happened to her eyes?"

Shane grimaced.

"Man up," Harley called from across the room. "This is part of the job."

"What would you know about it?" Shane shot back.

Wyatt pushed away from the wall and strode toward the whiteboard, his gaze roaming over the women's faces. "Harley has experience with this sort of work."

"What sort?" Sky whispered.

"Stalkers, serial killers, drug cartels, you name it, babe," Harley piped in.

Shane tilted his head. "CIA?"

"FBI."

"Great, a Fed."

"Former Fed, thank you. Can we return to the issue at hand? I believe Sky asked a question. And this time, don't punk out, Sheriff."

With a pinched expression, Shane turned back to her. "When we arrived on scene, the victim's eyes had been removed."

She froze.

"Were there any marks on the body to suggest trauma around the eyes?" Harley pressed.

"There were marks. The medical examiner couldn't conclusively determine the source."

Sky's stomach churned. A wave of nausea slammed into her, but if everyone else could hold themselves together, so would she. "But these photos..."

"Once a body is identified, families of the victims often provide us with personal information, such as photographs, that can be released to the public." Which was how they knew the victims were all blue-eyed. Sky nodded and digested that information.

"And as I previously stated," he continued, "it was assumed to have been the work of the wildlife. Until Erica Marsters arrived on the scene."

Shane tapped the middle photo, attracting Sky's attention. She felt as though she was looking at her future visage. Slight laugh lines crinkled the corners of her eyes and mouth, her blue eyes sparking with a hint of wisdom. The woman had to be in her late thirties and was drop-dead gorgeous.

"Erica Marsters was found within a mile of Humming Creek two weeks later, buried beneath the foliage. Unlike Barbara, Erica's body showed signs of a struggle. Had it not been for her eyes, the two cases might never have been connected." Shane's face crumpled. "DNA was found beneath her fingernails. It was a match."

Sky forced herself to swallow the bile rising in her throat. "To the samples from my windowsill?"

Shane nodded. "Unfortunately, this person isn't in the database, so even though we know it's the same person, we don't know who he is."

"You should have warned me," she whispered. They'd spoken on the phone this afternoon in the airport. He'd insisted she wait for an escort, but had he said why...

"Sky, the last thing I wanted was to upset you any further."

"She had a right to know, Mr. County Mounty." Harley crossed the room. "The moment the DNA came back as a match, you should have been on the wire alerting anyone and everyone. Now, you have a serial killer on your hands."

The world pitched to the side, and Sky reached out, her hand colliding with the desk for balance.

"Hindsight is great, and all that," Shane grumbled.

"Lack of experience, is more like."

"Enough," Wyatt grumbled. "No point crying over it, now."

"Why the eyes?" Sky whispered, interrupting what she was sure would lead to another pissing contest. Her attention skipped to each of them, but none seemed willing to speak up. "Why?"

"We don't know," Shane finally answered. "It's hard to say. Some murderers like to collect... souvenirs."

She shuddered, her mind taking a giant leap to a dark room teeming with gouged eyeballs stored in preservation jars. "You know what, forget I asked." She pressed a hand to her churning stomach.

"Tell us about the third body." Wyatt led the conversation down a separate path.

"Jody Anne Davidson, our most recent, and by far the most violent case."

Sky stared at the third picture. Another beautiful woman, forever memorialized in a photo, stared back. Her lush lips curved in a gentle smile, her dark blue eyes shimmering with laughter. Absolutely breathtaking, and Sky felt her gut twist when she realized that the woman's family would never lay eyes on her lovely face again.

"We called Wyatt in when we found Jody Anne. The marks on her torso suggest he's losing control. Having an alpha on the team is—"

"Convenient," Wyatt returned with a snarl.

"What marks?" Sky brought the conversation back on

target. She wasn't sure she wanted to hear the answer, but she had to know what they were dealing with. She couldn't hide in the dark anymore.

The room fell silent until finally Harley said, "Show her. She deserves to see."

"No," Wyatt ordered, the clipped word echoing through the room.

"Alpha, she deserves to know what's happening," Harley urged in a softer voice. "If we don't prepare her, any number of things could go wrong. She has to understand the magnitude of the situation."

Wyatt faced him, his eyes hard.

Sky's wide eyes bounced between the two of them. Harley stood two inches taller than the alpha, yet lacked the intimidation Wyatt conjured with his pinky finger. There was no doubt in her mind who would win in a fight, and it seemed Harley knew it. Former fed or not, he would obey his alpha.

Sick of the grandstanding, Sky planted her hands onto her hips and faced Shane—the only human in the room. "I decide what I can and cannot handle. Answer my question, now." The men weren't the only dominant wolves in the house. Perhaps it was time for her to show them she was made of more than sugar and spice.

"Skylar—"

"Shane. Now." Yup, she was beyond angry. Regardless of her emotional state, he had no reason to keep such a thing hidden from her. Not when she was top-of-the list for this psycho.

Shane's eyes flicked to Wyatt's, and Sky bristled. "No one asked the alpha," she snapped.

"If she's so desperate to see, let her."

There was a challenge in his voice, one that stiffened Sky's back. They didn't think she could handle it. And here she thought she'd been doing well. Resigned, she gave a terse nod and waited as Shane dug the photographs out of the folder. No matter what condition the body was in, she wouldn't retch, or so she told herself.

Shane withdrew the photo and laid it flat on Wyatt's desk. A shredded woman took shape before her eyes, the flesh on her chest sliced to ribbons. The first sharp breath didn't come from her; in fact, it came from Axel, who until that moment had held his statuesque position near the desk.

Sky's chin trembled, but she snapped her eyes closed and drew in a steady breath. No, the room was not swimming, and no the temperature had not spiked. It was all in her head. And she could control that. "Was he..." Her voice wavered and she cleared her throat, determined not to fail herself. "Was he in wolf form when he did that?"

"I don't know, but if I understand correctly, some werewolves can control individual body parts."

Wyatt grunted his assent.

"It's possible he only shifted his hands, *querida*," Bale murmured from across the room. "But he'd need to be an alpha to possess that level of control."

"Did he—" Sky choked on her words and pointed toward the picture. "Uh, did he...violate her?"

The silence in the room was answer enough. Her knees buckled and she dropped into Wyatt's computer chair.

"The other two, as well?"

"I'm sorry, Sky." Shane's palms curled over her shoulders, his reaction her answer. "But I swear, this guy won't lay a finger on you."

She flicked another glance to the image, her clammy palms curling into tight fists at the sight of Jody Anne's ruined torso. He'd raked his claws down her length, shredded her from neck to groin. She noticed something odd, and pressed a fist against her mouth to keep from losing what little food she'd eaten all day.

"Sky?"

She squeezed her eyes shut and forced her gaze away. "That's my nightgown she's wearing."

"What?" Shane's hands vanished from her shoulders as he scrambled to snatch up the photo.

The front of the slip was ruined, but she knew her own blue satin negligee. She'd bought it at the insistence of a friend, all the while knowing no one would ever see it. She was far too invested in her career to let a man slip into her life.

"How do you know?" Wyatt's deep voice rumbled behind her.

Her wolf ached for comfort, even if it meant leaning into him and taking whatever he could provide. Instead, she straightened in the chair and pointed to the image. "Down toward the thigh. I spilled a little bleach on it when I was doing a load of laundry." Her eyes narrowed in on the colorless spot. It'd broken her heart when it had happened. "Must have made her put it on while he was in my house."

The others fell into a stunned silence, and Sky took

that moment to glance at Wyatt. Violence brewed in the golden depth of his eyes, his mouth a ferocious line that promised retribution. Such a fierce stare might have terrified her, except for once, Sky found herself on common ground with him. Emboldened by the realization, she didn't argue when he pulled her out of the chair and drew her flush against him, the tips of his fingers settling against her waist.

"I vote we waste this guy," Harley suggested.

So preoccupied by the photo, not a single one of them had noticed the slight change between Sky and Wyatt, and she was content with that. She succumbed to her need and leaned into him, holding this newfound camaraderie close and using his strength to bolster her own.

"There is no vote," Wyatt snarled against her, his grip tight. "The fucker's dead."

## 10

A polite knock rapped against the kitchen doorframe. Focused on the amber liquid swirling within his glass, Wyatt grunted an invitation.

Harley crossed the room and dropped onto the stool next to him. "Those reporters are bloody annoying."

Wyatt nodded. "They've been calling me every hour, demanding an exclusive with Skylar."

"Parasites. They're camped out in the street, waiting to get a few candid shots of the werewolf advocate and the alpha."

Wyatt groaned. "That's what they're going to call us too."

Harley chuckled. "I did, however, just get off the phone with my contact in the bureau."

"Great. What do we know?" Wyatt demanded.

"What? No 'Thank you, Harley, for going out of your way to find this information'?"

Wyatt's lip curled over his teeth.

Harley blew out a harsh sigh and draped his arms over the table. "All right, I'm going to ask you something, even though you're probably going to kick my ass. Just remember that you like me and it would piss you off if I died."

"That's debatable."

"You'd weep," Harley informed him. "I don't doubt it."

"Ask the fucking question," he snarled.

Harley drew in a deep breath. "Here goes. What's going on with you? You've been a sour apple the past couple of days, and you and Sky have been actively avoiding one another."

Wyatt lifted his attention from the glass and leveled Harley with a murderous stare.

"Yup, regretting asking already. Remember...I'm your favorite."

Harley wasn't entirely wrong. It'd been two days since he'd brought Sky into his house, and it'd been a living nightmare. Seemed the Fates were getting a kick out of torturing him. He'd sworn to keep his distance, and instead, the bitches kept throwing them together. Felt like any time he went anywhere, there she was. If it wasn't the kitchen or the game room, then it was the hallway. Yesterday he'd woken up early to sneak in a shower only to find she'd had the same thought. There he'd stood in the washroom, forced to smell her shampoo and body wash. Needless to say, the towel rack hadn't survived his anger. Everywhere he fucking went, she was there. As though his wolf needed another reason to howl.

He had no intentions of discussing this with any of them. "What information did you find?"

With a sigh, Harley reached for the scotch bottle between them and poured his own glass. "You know, I'm not an FBI agent anymore. Going to them for trivial things like this really doesn't look good on me. A little appreciation—"

Wyatt's snarl echoed through the kitchen. He lifted the crystal to his lips and tossed back the scotch. "Do *not* make me ask again."

"There really wasn't much to find. No priors, no arrests, hell, the woman doesn't even have a speeding ticket under her name. One of my buddies put in a few calls to Sky's university. Seems she's rather popular among the faculty and student body. She's not the first werewolf to seek out post-secondary education, but she *is* the first in her field. Her Master's is in whatever the hell *Werewolf Sociocultural Evolutionism* is, and she's currently working on a Ph.D. in some other werewolf shit. I don't know, man, it was a lot of fancy words, and my brain isn't big enough to comprehend them all."

With a sigh, Wyatt spun the glass in his hand.

"I was given a courteous warning, though. The feds will be sending someone to check this out. Three deaths—"

"Makes a serial killer."

Harley's head bobbed. "They won't bother us, much. They'll want a statement from Sky, but they'll mostly be Shane's headache."

"Sky's given Shane her statement. That will suffice."

"Uh—"

Wyatt shot Harley a sharp glare.

"Right." Harley reached for his cell. "I'll give them a head's up, not that they'll listen. Meanwhile, I think our best lead is her old pack."

"And the sheriff," Wyatt said.

"Shane?"

Wyatt nodded. "The calls and letters stopped once he moved in."

"So? Maybe he scared the pervert off."

"You ever known an alpha werewolf to give up on something they want?"

Harley shot Wyatt with a sardonic stare. "Gee, let me think..."

Wyatt growled. He didn't want to think about his own problems right now. "Watch yourself."

"The sheriff is human, remember?"

He shrugged and poured another drink. "Wouldn't be the first time a werewolf has played human. It takes effort, but it can be done."

"What a conniving bastard," Harley said, sarcastically. "He starts with the phone calls, then starts hand-delivering creepy letters. But that's not enough. No, he's so obsessed with her, that he actually jerks off on her window-sill—which, gross. Not exactly the way to a girl's heart. *Then*, when she seeks out help, he offers his assistance. But wait, there's more. The guy actually moves into her house...and," Harley fed him wide eyes, "maintains a platonic relationship. What a bastard. Of course, we can't forget that during *all* this, he's pretending to be human." He gave a slow clap. "This guy is my hero."

Wyatt shook his head.

"You just don't like the guy."

"Sure don't," Wyatt agreed. "Doesn't change my mind, though. You agree it's a possibility?"

"Well, sure." Harley stressed the word. "He could be hiding that he's a werewolf. He could be obsessed with Sky, but then why wouldn't he try something with her? I'm sure they spent many quiet nights together."

Wyatt clenched the glass, the glass cracking at the edge.

"Ease up there, boss. Plucking glass out of flesh isn't fun."

He forced his fingers straight.

"If you like the girl, why not do something about it?"

He let out a ragged snarl. "Back off."

Harley gave a mock salute and then rose from his stool. Cupboard doors opened and closed as he pulled out the ingredients to make his renowned inch-thick peanut butter and jam sandwich. "It still seems to me that we should be looking into her old pack. Before her mother's funeral, everything was all hunky-dory. Mama bites the dust, daughter goes home for funeral, and bam... got yourself a stalker. Classic."

Wyatt arched a brow. "Really, *classic*?"

His third-in-command snatched a giant bite, speaking around a hunk of peanut butter. "Nah, but it sounds better than some-freak-starts-plucking-out-eyeballs, doncha think?"

"Charming. Tell me again how you're single?"

"Why, you wanna take a spin on the Harley?" He waggled his eyebrows, his olivine eyes sparkling with amusement. "And here I thought you preferred blondes."

"Hair color doesn't matter to me. But I do prefer my dates without balls," Wyatt responded dryly.

Harley choked on his sandwich, his face burning as brightly as his hair. "Nice one, Alpha. And where is our illustrious guest?"

Wyatt drained the glass. "Upstairs."

"Not that you're watching her or anything, hey?"

So not a topic he cared to discuss. "Top me up, will you?"

"The bottle's a couple inches from your hand."

"Mm, perks of being the alpha."

Harley scoffed under his breath and crossed the room with the remaining half of his sandwich. "And don't you just *love* to lord that over us."

"Don't like it? Challenge me at the next new moon."

Sarcastic laughter rumbled from Harley's throat. "Please, I like my heart right where it is, all alive and beating in my chest. I remember the last fight you were in. Gave me nightmares."

"Good." Wyatt lifted his hand and jingled the empty glass. "Then top me up."

The two joined in laughter as Harley filled the glass one inch at a time.

"You're pushing your luck, pup," Wyatt grumbled.

"So how many more drinks till you go upstairs and woo the lady?"

Wyatt froze, his gaze locked on the shimmering glass. For two days his wolf had been demanding the same thing. The feel of her body against his had been too good to forget, but he knew his wolves—meddlesome creatures that they were. The moment they spotted their alpha with a female, the bets were on. "Drop it."

"The bottle? Sure." He let it slip back to the counter. "Doesn't answer my question, though."

Wyatt growled. "Get used to disappointment."

Harley sighed and plopped back into the stool, his sandwich forgotten in light of the newest conversation. "I don't see what the problem is. Clearly, you like her."

A disgruntled laugh scraped past his lips. "Like her? She's the most infuriating woman I've ever met." And by far the sexiest.

"You're the only one who thinks so."

Wyatt scowled. "What are you talking about?"

"How can someone who watches her that closely be so blind?" Harley turned, the humor vanishing the moment he caught sight of Wyatt's face. Clearing his throat, he twisted the bottle of scotch between his hands. "Everyone adores her, especially Trinity."

Trinity...Wyatt blinked. She was one of his submissive wolves. Interesting that a dominant female like Sky would befriend one of the weakest in his pack. Not that he minded. His pack functioned well because his wolves treated each other with respect.

"I'm serious, boss. You think we didn't see you two clutching at each other up in your office a couple days ago? Not to mention that you both reek of frustration and desire."

"I can't begin to express how much this is *not* your business."

"It's all our business." He held up his hands and

instantly dropped his chin and gaze when Wyatt snatched at the bottle with a ferocious snarl. "Alpha. Think about it, all right? We all knew something was up the moment we stepped into that sickeningly sweet house of hers. You two are circling each other like alley cats, ready to tear into each other. My recommendation—"

"You're putting your life at risk, boy."

"—is go up there, get your fuck on, and wash your hands of each other so we can focus on the case."

"*Harley*," Wyatt barked. "Enough. I don't want to hear another word."

Harley's gaze dipped to Wyatt's clenched fist, and he nodded before taking another bite of his sandwich, cramming his gullet with peanut butter. At least it would shut him up. Wyatt stretched out his fingers and then pushed to his feet and started for the stairwell. What would it hurt to check in on her and ensure she was settling in well enough?

He climbed the stairs without preamble, noting Harley's presence behind him. The truth was, he would have liked nothing more than to *get his fuck on* as Harley had put it. Sky had wormed her way under his skin with that right hook. His jaw still remembered the feel of her knuckles crashing into him, and it brought a dangerous smile to his lips. Would she be as aggressive in bed? He dared to hope so.

He turned the corner and jerked to a stop. Harley stumbled into his back, his muttered complaint dropping off the moment he caught sight of the sheriff bent over Sky, mouth pressed against hers. A burst of white-hot fury twisted Wyatt's gut, rousing his wolf awake.

"Son-of-a-bitch," Harley choked on a shocked laugh. "Someone's dead meat."

"What the fuck is he doing here?" Wyatt's voice echoed in the hallway. They had protocols in place for a reason. No one entered his house without his permission.

Shane stiffened, his gaze flicking to Wyatt's before he straightened. "Uh, I'll be leaving now."

"I think I'll walk you out," Harley offered. "Make sure you get there in one piece."

The sheriff brushed past Wyatt, and it took every ounce of restraint not to let his wolf rip into the bastard. As it was, he kept his eyes forward and locked on Sky, whose distressed gaze spoke louder than words.

---

*Shane kissed me.*

She couldn't stop the echo as her mind repeated that sentiment over and over. He'd kissed her, like full on grabbed her, dragged her close, and kissed her. And in the middle of Wyatt's hallway.

*Wyatt.*

Sky blinked and met his bright stare. At the sight of his wolf, her own woke and stretched, intrigued by the situation. She waited for him to move toward her, or speak, or something, but he stood at the end of the hall, still as stone, fists clenched at his sides.

"Well, I'm not going to apologize, if that's what you're waiting for," she uttered before turning toward her door. Not that she had anything to apologize for. It wasn't as though she'd asked Shane to kiss her. They'd been discussing her thesis, and then he'd swooped in. Somehow, he'd managed to keep his emotions hidden from her. But the moment his mouth brushed hers, the warm scent of desire smacked her in the face. Not for the first time, she found herself grateful he wasn't a werewolf. Otherwise, he would have known right then that the attraction wasn't mutual.

"Are you two together?" Wyatt's voice sounded odd, distant almost, as though he was struggling for control.

"I—I...uh..." She peered around him to see if Shane was still nearby.

"Well?" A shot of anger darkened his tone.

Sky lifted her chin and met his piercing stare. Through the dark hall, all she could make out was his silhouette and the burn of his eyes. It was enough to elicit a shiver.

"You know, that's not really any of your business." She reached for the door handle, intent on escaping.

"You make a shitty couple."

She froze, her hand on the brass knob. So close. "Excuse me?" She whirled around, her hand darting to her throat when she found him only inches away.

"I'd wager you're not."

She blinked. "Not what?"

"Together."

Was he still on that? "What makes you say so?"

He stepped flush against her, and with a hitched breath, Sky darted backward, his arms caging her against the wall. Now...why was this so familiar? Ah, right...her thoughts conjured the memory of them together in the stairwell of her house, his rough hands sliding down her body as he kissed the hell out of her.

"No connection."

She pushed away the memory and tipped her head up. "What?"

Wyatt leaned in close until she could feel his breath on her face. "You and Shane," he murmured, the sweet scent of scotch hitting her nose, "have no connection. See, there are important components needed for a successful kiss."

Sky's gaze dipped to his sinful mouth, her heart lurching.

"There needs to be passion, an unquenchable desire for one another." His husky voice awakened something in her that Shane had failed to.

Her tongue flicked out and dampened her lips.

"There has to be heat and hunger."

Oh, God, her knees turned to jelly.

"In other words, darling, the kiss needs to get you hot, needs to make you wet." He angled in close and brushed his mouth along her jaw. "Hear your heartbeat right now? Feel that craving deep in your bones? That's lust, baby. And Shane doesn't have what it takes to make you come." He leaned back, her chin captured between his fingers as he caught her gaze. "But I do."

*Sweet Lord.* Heat spread through her limbs, her body reacting viscerally to his words. The memory of his lips against hers emboldened her, dared her to take the next step. Wyatt was a dick, but he didn't pretend to be otherwise. She respected that. With all the madness in her life, would it be so bad to take something for herself?

"Is that so?" she whispered, loosening the reins on her wolf. "Then what are you waiting for?"

His mouth curved upward into a sexy grin that stole her breath. "It's your turn, darling."

*My turn?* It took a second for her to realize his meaning. He'd initiated the last kiss; he wanted her to take the lead this time. And why the hell did that turn her on? With a quiet growl, she climbed the length of his body in a race to reach him, and the moment their mouths clashed, she melted into him.

His hands were everywhere, his mouth hard and demanding. Surrendering to the emotions he inspired, she met him with equal abandon and devoured his mouth. This time she refused to stand meekly by as he licked and teased her, this time she meant to give as good as she got, and oh baby, was it good. Heat flared in her stomach as his fingers kneaded her thighs before he lifted her into the air. The hard press of the wall against her back and the heat between her legs made her heart pound.

He tore his mouth from hers and gazed up at her. He reached up and unbound her hair, his breath sharp when it fell in a golden curtain around her face. "See? Connection. My room is down the hall."

"Too far," she whispered, nipping at the shell of his ear. "My room is right here."

"Your room," he grunted, "won't have condoms."

"I'm on the pill."

He groaned and leaned his head against her chest. "You're going to kill me."

"That's the plan."

Cupping her ass, he wrenched her away from the wall and swept into her room, kicking the door shut behind them. He staggered to the bed and dropped her down onto the mattress, his palms sliding beneath her shirt.

When his hand found her bare breast, he pulled back and stared down on her. "You're not wearing a bra."

She grinned at him. "Nope."

He swallowed and glanced down her length, his brow winging up at the sight of her sparkling navel ring. "Yeehaw," he muttered before pushing up her shirt and running his thumbs over her pert nipples. She shivered beneath him, her own hands fumbling with his belt. She'd never felt such a need to remove a man's pants, and damn her fingers for not obeying.

He chuckled against her. "Need some help there, darling?"

Her eyes crossed when he bent over her and took her nipple into his hot mouth, tongue laving over the sensitive nub. "No," she gasped and then rejoiced when his belt came apart in her hands. The button slipped open next without an issue. Her fingers fell to the zipper, her breath hitched with anticipation when a sudden beam of light spilled over them.

"Sky, I wanted to make sure—"

"What the fuck!" Wyatt shouted as he threw the covers over Sky's bare chest.

"Jesus, Shane! Don't you knock?" Sky drew in a shuddering breath. Embarrassment flooded her cheeks as she hid beneath the thick quilt.

"Get the fuck out," Wyatt roared.

"I, uh—," Shane stuttered. "I didn't think—"

"No, you didn't think!"

"Wyatt," Sky snapped, the back of her hand slapping against his arm. "Ease up." But his wolf was unleashed, she saw it in his amber gaze, heard it in the savage rumble of his voice. "Shane, you should go," she whispered, fear worming into her chest at the sight of Wyatt's fractured control.

But the sheriff didn't budge an inch. "Sky, I thought..." His voice trailed. "I don't know what I thought, but I didn't expect you to fall into his bed."

She bristled. "I fell into my bed, thank you very much."

Wyatt rose from the bed, all six foot four of him. He looked demonic, standing in the dark, his eyes blazing as he glared at Shane. "She's mine."

Two words, and they doused the flames within her. "Excuse me?" she demanded in a cold voice.

Wyatt spared her a quick glance, his lips curled back over newly-sprouted fangs.

Yanking her shirt down, she shoved the blankets back and rose from the bed, indifferent to her current state. "Let's get something clear, buddy. And this goes for the both of you. I'm not anybody's. Least of all yours, Wyatt Turner. I'm not some possession for you to claim, mark, and then lead around on your arm like some trophy wife."

"You're my mate."

"I haven't agreed to that!"

Part of her feared his reaction. Alpha that he was, he clearly wasn't used to being denied what he wanted. But

Sky had sworn that she would never allow any man to do what her former alpha had done to his pack. The women there were little more than docile puppies. Straightening her back, she squared her shoulders and jabbed a finger toward the door. "Out, both of you."

"Sky—"

"Get. Out. Right now, Wyatt, or so help me—"

"What?" He pushed into her space. "What are you going to do if I don't leave?"

She couldn't force him physically, but there was one tool she had in her arsenal that she knew would frighten Wyatt off. With her next breath, she summoned a fresh batch of tears, watching as he stiffened in front of her.

"Aw, hell, woman. I didn't mean...I—"

"Leave, Wyatt." She added a slight shiver to her voice.

"Sky..." he groaned, his eyes dimming as his wolf receded, "you're killing me, don't cry."

She turned away and buried her face in her hands before he sensed that she was forcing them. It wasn't entirely difficult to do so, a lot had happened in the past few days, and her emotions were unstable as it was. "Get out!"

She felt the light graze of his hand against her hair before he vacated, bellowing for Harley to get his ass up the stairs. And when the door clicked shut, she sucked back the tears and dropped down onto the bed.

"I'm not his fucking keeper!" she heard Harley grumble in the hallway. "I thought he left!"

Sky rolled her eyes and buried her head into her

pillow. Unfortunately, her body was still wound up, and with no outlet...she grunted in frustration and stared at her small bag. There was absolutely nothing in there that would help.

Cold shower, it was.

## 11
---

Sky stirred when gentle fingers caressed the side of her neck. Half-asleep, she moaned and sank into the pillows, drawing out the comforting touch. A low purr slipped from her lips, and her exhausted body unwound after a fitful night's sleep.

*Last night.*

Her eyes snapped open, her heart skipping a beat at the sight of Wyatt crouched next to her bed, his thumb lazing across her collarbone. "Morning."

She swallowed her greeting, afraid to speak lest he get a whiff of morning breath. Horrified, she covered her mouth and jerked up. The corners of his mouth tugged, and his gaze drifted over her.

*Oh, God, my hair!*

She wasn't in any state to see anyone. "Wyatt..."

A damn grin stretched over his face, stopping her heart dead. "I wanted to show you what you could have woken up next to this morning."

And didn't she know it? There he crouched, groomed and kempt, and finer than all hell, while she looked—and felt—like a nightmare. She quickly palmed away any drool and then smoothed her hands down her hair.

"I'm touched that you want to look your best for me. But I must say..." he leaned forward and brushed a stray hair behind her ear, "you're sexy no matter what you look like, Sky."

Her brows deepened. What was he playing at? Before last night, he hadn't given her the time of day since the meeting in the office. So, what? *Now* he wanted her? Still hiding behind her hand, she flicked a glance to the door, noting that it stood open. "Do you need something?"

"You." He said it so assuredly that she turned and blinked at him.

"Me? Why?" She didn't care what her wolf thought—she'd spent years suppressing her baser instincts. Just because her wolf cried *mate* didn't mean she would succumb.

With another smile, he pushed off his thighs and stood. Her gaze climbed his length, cheeks burning when she lingered over his blasted belt buckle.

"I didn't want to wake you, but this couldn't wait any longer. We have to go."

"Go?" She lowered her hands to the blanket and fiddled with the edge. "Go where?"

His mouth twisted. "You're not going to like it."

"Go *where*?" she demanded.

"To Hidden Creek."

Her stomach shot up into her throat. "Uh, no."

"Uh, *yes*."

Skylar shoved down the blankets and kneeled in the middle of the bed. "Wyatt, I swore I would never go back there. There's absolutely no reason—"

He bowed over the bed, the heady scent of werewolf overwhelming her. "Ah, but there are reasons." He held up a single finger. "This all began with your mother's funeral. Your pack is likely the origin." He flicked up a second finger. "It gets you out of town for a few days while Shane and my men investigate the murders." A third finger rose as did the corner of his mouth. "Gives us a chance to get to know each other."

She swallowed. "I thought you didn't want to get to know me."

He shot her a droll stare. "I never said that, and after last night—"

"Last night was a mistake!" she stammered. "Things got out of hand."

Gold rimmed his irises.

"Can't we phone them?" she asked, grasping at any straw she could find.

He gave a dark and edgy laugh. "Sure, I bet your pack will be more than accommodating."

"I don't have any say in this, do I?"

"Sky..." He grasped her chin and lifted it until she blinked at him. "I know this is hard for you, but there have been three murders in the past six months. I refuse to sit back and wait for the next attack. If this jackass is from your old pack, we need to find out."

She grimaced. "Why are you being nice to me, now?"

"Maybe I want to show you there's more to me than an asshole."

Her watery chuckle broke the tension. "Well, stop it, it's freaking me out."

Wyatt laughed—truly *laughed*—for the first time since they'd met. "Don't forget that you were the one who put a stop to it."

Unnerved, she crawled off the bed and reached for her bag. "Yeah, yeah. Can I at least shower before we leave?"

He gave a playful wink, and with a grunt, pointed toward the door down the hall. Then with a true growl, he nodded toward her bare legs. "But put on some damn pants before you leave the room. It would be tragic if I had to kill someone for checking you out before we leave."

She gazed down her length, her cheeks burning when she realized she stood in the middle of the room in nothing more than a thin T-shirt and a thong.

---

"You can't expect her to ride bitch for eight hundred miles," Bale grumbled as the stepped in the garage. "The woman is positively green around motorcycles."

Wyatt snapped an irritated glare at his second. Bale had latched onto him the moment Sky stepped into the shower, needlessly voicing his concerns about the plan. He had yet to let up, and it was driving Wyatt insane. "I expect her to do as she's told. Same goes for the rest of you. Harley will be working closely with Shane and the fed, while you and Axel are to increase security here."

Maybe he was an asshole, but it made him a good alpha—strong and unwilling to compromise. With a pack of sixty-eight, he refused to sacrifice that trait. At the first hint of weakness, those waiting in the wings would pounce and rip him to shreds. *Nice* wasn't something he could afford. The fact that Sky understood that turned him on like nothing else. Somehow he knew there would be no need to compromise anything with her.

"Alpha—"

Wyatt growled, his lips curled back. "Enough. I've allowed you to speak your mind. You've been overruled."

His second snapped to attention and gave a sharp nod, though fire still burned in his eyes.

Soft footsteps drew his attention to the doorway where Sky entered. Her gaze flicked to his bike. "No, oh, no, no, no..."

She'd responded much the same way the first time she'd laid eyes on *Monster*, the bike he'd owned since he'd become the alpha. When he'd taken the position, he'd needed *something* to distract him from the politics and squabbles. So, he'd purchased a rundown bike from a scrapyard and slowly rebuilt it. The time it'd taken had reminded him how good it felt to work with his hands.

"Don't you have a car or something?"

The panic in her voice furrowed his brows. What was she so frightened of? She'd ridden it before. But when she stomped past him, the sharp scent of desire and dread clouded his nose. With a wicked grin, he leaned over and whispered in her ear, "Don't worry, you can hold onto me the entire way."

Her faint whimper encouraged him.

He handed her a pair of leather chaps, the closest in size he could find. "Put these on."

She cocked a brow. "You know how long a drive it is to California, right?"

He hummed his assent.

"Have you ever ridden a motorcycle for that long?"

"Cross country," he informed her, taking a moment to reminisce.

"Well, I haven't!"

"Time to experience it then, isn't it?"

She crossed her arms over her chest and tapped her foot. "Remember when I said to stop being so nice?"

He flashed her another grin. He couldn't help it, she was just so damn amusing this morning. "Mhmm."

"Well, I take it back."

"Too late, darling."

He gestured toward the chaps once more and waited patiently as she struggled to pull them on. Then he handed her a leather jacket that was a size too large, but it would have to do. The helmet came next, and he chuckled at her dismayed expression as he put it on and cinched the chin strap. He stood back, his libido stirring at the sight of Sky sheathed in leather. The blonde hair stood apart from the rest, but he liked it—his own Biker Barbie.

With a terse nod, he looked to Bale. "You're in charge while I'm away. Don't let them walk all over you. If you need to put them in their place, do it. Don't hesitate. I will have my cell on me the entire time. Call me for any emergencies."

"Yes, Dad," Bale drawled. He sauntered over to Sky and knocked on her helmet. "Ride safe. Don't lean into the turns with him, and tell him if you need to stop."

"Yes, Dad," Sky mimicked him.

Wyatt chuckled and hopped onto his seat, waiting until Sky's weight settled in behind him before he fired up the engine. When he did, her arms slipped around his sides, her hands pressed flat against his chest. He glanced down at her nimble fingers, only now realizing how challenging this ride was going to be. Pressed tightly against each other on a machine that vibrated for both his and her pleasure...he shook his head and looked to Bale.

"Harley took a peek outside and, sadly, the crowd has grown," Bale shouted over the engine. "There's no way to avoid them, and you can't drive through them, so be careful. Axel and I will be out there to ensure no one gets injured during your getaway. Give us a few minutes to get out there, and then you're cleared to leave."

"Crowd? What crowd?" Sky demanded once Bale sauntered out of the garage.

"Stupid reporters," Wyatt sighed. "They've been camped out there for two days. How they knew you were here, I don't know. Harley is looking into it. We'll be careful."

And with that, he revved the engine, grinning when Sky squealed and pressed herself flush against him. Nothing like a bike ride on a beautiful day, with a gorgeous woman plastered against his back. This was going to be a blast.

He leaned back and watched as the garage door slid open and a flood of hungry reporters descended upon Wyatt and Sky. His lip curled as he glared at the fucking alpha, all kingly as he rode out on the piece of shit he'd dubbed *Monster*.

He *hated* him like no other. The jackass actually thought himself an alpha. He was nothing but a thug—a grease monkey who had struck gold by landing himself a weak pack with an even weaker alpha. The asshole had ripped out his former alpha's heart, and they'd fucking *cheered* as though he was some god. He was no god—he was a thief who had taken something that hadn't belonged to him.

And now Wyatt was doing it again, stealing something not his.

Sky was *his*. His wolf wouldn't allow it any other way. All he'd needed was a few more minutes of her time to show her how good they could be together. A few more minutes without that fucking alpha breathing down her neck.

Then he would finally have her. Wyatt thought he was so clever, keeping her under lock and key, but the fucker didn't have a clue who he was messing with. The idiot couldn't see ten feet in front of his face, let alone the vultures that encircled him.

His burning gaze narrowed on the sight of Sky's body flush against Wyatt. He pushed out of his vehicle with a snarl, kicking the door shut hard enough for it to dent. It wasn't supposed to be like this! He grasped at the roots of his hair and pulled, the sharp pain enough to return his senses.

*No*, he would not give in so easily. He would have his mate, and he would destroy anything—or *anyone*—that stood in his way. The alpha thought he was tough? They'd see how tough he was with a silver bullet drilled into this heart.

His mouth curled with the violent thought, pleasure warming his gut.

"Are you waiting to speak with the alpha?" a docile voice rose next to him.

He turned, his mouth morphing into a predatory grin at the sight of the petite werewolf standing next to him, her light brown eyes gentle and trusting. How sad that Wyatt had left those reliant on him alone and without protection.

Golden hair spilled over her shoulders, framing a tender face that reminded him of a young Sky. His cock thickened at the sight of her, the proverbial lamb left to the slaughter. *One more*, he promised himself, *to take the edge off and help me think.*

Next time, it would be Sky, right next to Wyatt's dead body.

## 12

Every bone ached.

Sky staggered away from *Monster* with a low groan. Never in her life had she been so uncomfortable. The eight hours it'd taken them to drive to California from Colorado had been insufferable. Thankfully, Wyatt had stopped now and then, so she could stretch her cramped legs.

Unkinking her knees, she placed her hands in the small of her back and worked out the knots. One advantage to living among humans was seeing how long it took their bodies to recuperate in comparison to werewolves. Right now, she was grateful that her sore muscles would be healed in a few hours as opposed to days.

Sky turned and swept her gaze across Hidden Creek. As expected, nothing had changed in the year since her mother's funeral.

"How's your ass?"

Blinking, Sky turned back to find Wyatt scoping out her butt. "Excuse me?"

"Your ass." He chuckled, unabashed. "Must be sore after that ride. Need a massage?"

Desire bloomed in her stomach, and her breath caught at the memory of his fingers kneading her thighs and caressing her breasts.

"I'd be more than happy to oblige." He stepped up next to her, mouth curled in a playful grin.

"Your mood swings are going to give me whiplash," she grumbled. "Yesterday you wouldn't have given me the time of day, then last night..."

"Last night, I saw something I didn't like."

She nibbled her bottom lip. "Shane's a friend."

"That dick's got more than friendship on his mind."

"So, now you want me."

He stepped forward, his gaze slowly climbing her length until it settled on her mouth. "Mhmm. Might as well accept it."

"Until you lose interest again." She shook her head.

"Not gonna happen." He stepped forward and hooked a finger under her chin. "I wasn't ignoring you because you bore me. Do I look bored to you?"

She swallowed and flicked a glance down. "Then why bother ignoring me in the first place?"

He chuckled as he traced his finger down her throat. "Because I'm an idiot."

"Now, that I believe." She lifted her head and caught his gaze. Time for a jolt of honesty. "I don't know if I want a mate." Last night, she would have said yes to anything Wyatt asked—including mating. But today, her doubts had once again reared their ugly head.

"Give me a chance to convince you." He leaned down and murmured in her ear, "I guarantee you'll enjoy it."

Desire drew her closer until his mouth brushed against her neck. He groaned and threaded his fingers through her hair, holding her still as he nipped at her flesh.

Sky cleared her throat and pushed away from him, her eyes locked on her feet. "I'll...uh...let you know."

"You do that."

He brushed past her and strode toward the hotel reception, no limp in sight. Sky shook her head and turned to study her hometown once more. It wouldn't be long before word spread like wildfire that she was back, and with an alpha in tow. She would have rather they not come, but Wyatt was right. She'd confessed in his office that it had all begun after the funeral. That was the connection. It made sense for it to be someone in her former wolf pack, but she couldn't imagine any of them straying away from Hidden Creek.

"Ready?"

She turned back toward the hotel. "That was quick. Did you get our rooms sorted out?"

"*Rooms*?" He lifted a brow over his still-blazing eyes.

Her gut burned at the sight of his quirked mouth. "Yes, *rooms*."

"No. But I did get our room, *singular*, sorted out."

She planted her hands on her hips. "Plural. We're not mates. We're not even dating. I am *not* staying the night with you in a hotel room." This was her hometown for crying out loud, a place her former alpha had ingrained with conservative values.

His brows knotted. "Actually, you are." He turned and started back toward the hotel, as though he expected her to follow.

Cursing under her breath, Sky knew she had to take this into her own hands. She stormed past Wyatt and stalked into the hotel lobby, her fuming gaze landing on the poor woman behind the desk, someone Sky had never met.

"Hi. I'd like my own room, please."

"What are you doing?" Wyatt's voice thundered through the entry.

Sky refused to flinch, but the human squeaked and stepped back as though expecting a showdown.

"I'm getting my own room." She turned and leaned against the desk, arms crossed over her chest. "Isn't that obvious?"

His gaze flicked over her head, and he addressed the receptionist. "No, she isn't."

A shot of anger tightened her muscles. She straightened out her hands and forced her body to relax. If *anything* was to happen between them, this alpha needed to learn a few lessons. No one spoke for her, not anymore. With a deep breath, she squared her shoulders and planted her feet wide apart, hands fisted on her hips. "Yes, I am." She turned back to the receptionist and slapped her card down on the counter. "This is me, paying for my own room. So, back off."

"Sky, I'm not going to keep arguing with you."

She bristled. "Good, maybe you'll get a clue."

Wyatt stalked toward her, leather boots clomping against the tile floor. "Need I remind you that you had *no* problem staying in a room with me last night? In fact, if your bloody sheriff hadn't shoved his nose in, I would have fucked you senseless."

The receptionist gasped, and Sky's jaw dropped.

"So, explain to me why we need separate rooms? Afraid?"

"That..." She stuttered, her mouth moving wordlessly as she struggled to find a retort. "You arrogant...*pig!*" She stammered out the final words, her cheeks burning. Tossing up her hands, she uttered a frustrated cry, spun back around, and shoved her card across the desk. "Get me my own room. And it better be as far from his as possible. I'm talking at least three levels between us."

"Sky—"

"And *you!*" She spun back toward him and jabbed a finger at him. "Come near me tonight, and I swear, you'll be hunting for your balls in the morning."

"Try it," he growled, hands grasping her upper arms.

Sky curled a lip and jerked out from under his touch. "Don't push me, Wyatt. I've taken about all I can handle from you. Room key, *now.*"

The human fumbled with the key, dropping it once before it finally made its way into Sky's palm.

"What room?" Sky demanded.

"Eight thirty-four," the woman whispered. "He's...uh, I gave him one-oh-four."

"Thank you."

Whirling on her heel, Sky stomped down the hall

and jabbed the elevator button.

"Sky, would you just—"

"No," she snarled. "I can't believe I agreed to this." The doors slid open, and Sky entered without so much as a glance in his direction. "Stay away from me," she barked out before punching the button that closed the doors.

"You are so infuriating!" he shouted as the doors began to close.

"Ditto!" she shot back.

The doors closed with a gentle swish of air. Sky sank back against the wall, her eyes fluttering shut as the elevator began its ascent. Heart pounding and blood pumping, every inch of her was coiled. She needed a run; her wolf demanded to be set free. She'd intended on inviting him for one tonight, but now...she growled and kicked at the wall. Had he simply *asked* her to room with him, they could have discussed why it wasn't such a great idea. It was the way he went about these things, all macho and demanding, without any thought to people's feelings.

It was her fault. She'd told him not to be nice. But had she known...*no*. She took a deep, cleansing breath. Anger wouldn't do anything but eat at her stomach, and an ulcer was not something she coveted. Also, approaching her family and pack angry wouldn't accomplish anything. A few hours alone in her room would help calm her rage.

Or so she thought.

The elevator dinged, and the doors slid open to reveal Wyatt standing there with his arms crossed over his massive chest. Eight floors, and he stood there as though dashing up that many stairs hadn't broken a sweat! Wanting to scream, Sky shoved past him, located her room, and slammed the door in his arrogant face.

"Keep me out all you want, Sky, but I'm not leaving this hallway."

Whatever calm she'd managed to find in the elevator all but evaporated.

"Infuriating!" she growled before slamming her bathroom door shut and turning on the bathtub faucets.

Like she'd ever mate with an asshole like him.

———

Wyatt disconnected from the call and stared down at his phone. A crack ran across the glass screen, one that hadn't been there ten minutes ago. But the moment Bale informed him of the most recent attack, his hand had tightened until the phone had shattered in his ear.

"Sky. Open up."

This news would devastate her. He remembered what Harley had told him, how Sky had bonded with Trinity. And now...

He sucked in a deep breath and dropped his head against her door. By his watch, three hours had passed since she'd locked him out. His legs had cramped up an hour back, and he'd taken to pacing, his ears quirked for any strange noises.

"Sky." This time he rapped gently against the door.

For crying out loud, this was not how he'd imagined tonight going down. After an entire day of her glorious body pressed against his, he'd wanted nothing more than to lock the door and screw her senseless. Now, he couldn't even get her to talk to him, not that he wanted to break her heart.

He knocked louder. "Sky!"

The door flung wide. "What?"

All right, so she was still angry—the sharp scent filled his nose and melted the wall of ice in his chest. Was he sick in the head for finding perverse satisfaction in the fact that he angered her?

He *liked* that he was the alpha, but there was something about Sky's reluctance to fall in place that turned him into a randy schoolboy. The challenge, the desire to dominate, the rush of adrenaline...

"Listen..." His words trailed off. Well, shit. What the hell was he supposed to tell her? *Man up*, Harley's voice boomed in his head. As the alpha it was his job to deliver bad news. But staring into her bright blue eyes, he wondered if he could do it this time.

She arched a thin brow, a spark of challenge blazing in her eyes. "Well?"

"Let me in."

"I'm not finished being angry with you."

He grunted. "I booked the single room because you shouldn't be alone. Damn it, Sky! There's a psychopath out there murdering women who look like you, and you want to be *alone*?" For fuck's sake, that was how the bastard had gotten his damned hands on Trinity. Wyatt refused to let that happen to Sky.

Her mouth slipped to the side. "So, you didn't have any ulterior motives?"

His brows snapped down. "'Course I did. What'd you expect?"

Sky uncrossed her arms and turned away from the door, heading back into her room. Well, she hadn't slammed the door in his face—progress, at least. Wyatt stalked forward and sealed them in the room with a click.

"If you'd only *asked* me..."

"For crying out loud, is *that* what this is about? Your feelings are hurt because I didn't *ask* first?"

She whirled around. "You know, you have a mighty fine way of apologizing."

"Apologizing for what, exactly? Wanting to protect you?"

An exasperated sound spilled from her lips. "For being so...*dominant!*"

Wyatt blinked at her. "You want me to apologize for being an alpha?"

"No!" She made another frustrated noise, heat rising to her cheeks. "It would have been nice if you'd asked me, first. Rather than treating me like some member of your pack who has to do what you say."

"So...you want me to apologize for being an alpha."

She sighed and turned to face the window.

Clearly, they weren't going to solve this problem tonight. "Listen, Sky." He raked a hand through his short hair and grimaced. *Tell her.* "Bale phoned."

She glanced over her shoulder, her thin brows knotting. "Something's wrong."

For Christ's sake, how was he going to do this? He dragged a hand down his face and nodded. "There's been another incident."

"Incident? What does that mean?"

He stepped forward and twined their hands together.

"You're scaring me," she whispered.

"Another victim." He drew her away from the window and toward the nearest chair. This wasn't going to be easy for her to hear. "The good news is that she survived."

Sky dropped into the chair with a heavy breath. "The victim *survived?*"

"The first three were all human. This time he went after another werewolf. Maybe he miscalculated, maybe he was in a rush, we don't know. But she survived, and maybe she'll be able to tell us who he is."

"Then what's the bad news?"

He squared his shoulders. *Like ripping off a Band-Aid.* "He blinded her. Just the others."

"Oh, my God." Sky slumped into the chair and covered her face with her hands. "Oh, my God." Her breath soughed past her fingers as she drew her knees into her chest and rocked into them. "Wait, a werewolf?" Her hands dropped from her face to reveal tear-stained cheeks. "All the werewolves in Colorado belong to you. Who was it?"

He hesitated.

"Who was it, Wyatt?"

"Trinity."

Her face crumpled with despair. She sucked in a sharp breath, her watery gaze dropping to her hands. "Trinity?"

Wyatt's gut twisted, his friggin' heart shattering into a million pieces as he watched her fall apart. He dropped to his knees before the chair and pulled her into his chest. "I'm so sorry, Sky."

"Will she be all right?"

He stoked her hair and nodded. "The doctors are optimistic. They did what they could for her. There will be some scarring, but she'll live."

Her fingers tangled in his shirt. "He must have known I was with you."

Wyatt's eyes fluttered shut, his jaw tight enough to fracture. That was Bale's estimation, as well. Thankfully, someone had stumbled across her and called the police. According to Shane's report, they'd thought Trinity was dead, but the paramedics on scene had managed to resuscitate her. "He'll never lay a finger on you, Sky. I swear."

"Don't make promises you can't keep," she whispered, her body still trembling against his. "He won't stop until he has me."

Wyatt dipped his head and met her gaze. "I will do everything in my power to keep you safe. That I can promise." He brushed her hair back from her damp cheek. "I doubt we'll always get along, Sky. Two dominant wolves tend to nip at one another. But I swear I will always protect you."

She gave a lifeless smile and pushed away from him. "I swore to myself that I would never take a mate."

Wyatt frowned, but held his tongue.

"I grew up in a pack that only cared about one thing. Tradition. When I left to pursue my interest in politics, I was exiled. I told myself I would never again be put in a position where I have to obey another. My pack tried to control me for most my life. I don't want that for myself, Wyatt."

"I understand that."

"Do you? Everything with you is orders."

He grimaced. "I can work on that, Sky. But you have to cut me some slack. I'm an alpha for a reason."

"And I'm a lone wolf for a reason, as well."

He nodded. "It won't be easy. But it's something we can tackle together, if you're willing."

"And what if it doesn't work? Will you understand if I want to leave?"

He swallowed his growl. His wolf howled a definitive *no*, but somehow, he guessed this was a make it or break it question. "You'll always be free to leave. But know that I will follow." He pushed onto his knees and slid his hands up her thighs. "Sky, take a chance on me."

She watched him with tears still fresh in her eyes. "Is now really the best time to discuss this?"

He shook his head. She was right. Right now, she needed comfort. "Come on," he murmured as he took her hand and led her toward the window.

"Where are we going?"

"For a run. Let's put everything out of our minds and lose ourselves to our wolves. Trinity will survive, and there's nothing we can do for her right now. Bale is with her."

Without waiting for an answer, he led her to the balcony and scaled down the eight flights of stairs. The moment his feet met the concrete pavement, he ripped off his shirt, threw it at her, and then dropped down onto all fours.

"You know we shouldn't shift in public, right?"

Her voice was weak, but he chuckled to himself, recalling how she'd worried over that before. Though it wasn't illegal for them to run through the streets, it was considered indecent exposure to remove their clothes before shifting.

"You're with the alpha," he teased, recalling the one time a police officer had tried to ticket him. By the end of the exchange, the officer was the one begging forgiveness. It was good to be the alpha. Few had the balls to stand up to him.

"Not the alpha of *this* territory."

He growled a nonsensical response, his words swallowed by his wolf. Distantly, he heard Sky's own grunts, and when he turned, he found a tawny wolf standing proud next to him, her head reaching his shoulder.

He'd already known her wolf form was as beautiful as her human side. Thick, multi-colored fur covered her from the tip of her nose to her tail, eyes bright and alive. Chuffing under his breath, Wyatt brushed against her side and then dashed off, knowing she would chase.

She trotted after him, her heart not quite in it. Wyatt yipped at her, then looped back and gently nipped at her side. For one night, he wanted to help her forget. He leapt about, playful as a pup, hoping to spark her wolf's interest. After a few blocks, he pounced and tugged on her ear until, finally, a flash of gold rimmed her eyes. *There she is...* his wolf threw his head back and howled.

Circling around him, she caught his shoulder between her teeth and then drove him toward the coast, her nose lifted in the air as though scenting something. With a final glance back, she bolted. A rush of adrenaline spurred Wyatt forward. If she wanted to race...

He tore after her, his lower jaw hanging open in a grin as they rushed toward the beach. Hidden Creek was nothing but a speck in the distance as the waves crashed nearby, the salty sea air ruffling their fur.

Now *this* was something he could grow accustomed to, and with a playful bark, one he hadn't uttered in years, he drove into Sky's side and licked her muzzle. She whirled around, shock brimming in her eyes before she grinned and dropped her front half down, her rear wiggling in the air.

Wyatt chuffed at the sight of her flicking tail. Though he already thought her beautiful, it was nothing compared to this moment, seeing her melded as one with her wolf. Her tawny fur shone in the moonlight, her sky blue eyes devoid of pain. In this moment, he knew he would do whatever it took to make her happy.

He stalked around her and nudged her shoulder with his, shoving her into the sea. She barked as she slipped under the waves, before coming up with a raking grin. Shaking out her fur, she eased farther into the water, taunting him until he followed.

Wyatt lost track of time as they frolicked in the ocean, tackling and splashing one another mercilessly. The salty sea clung to their fur, but neither cared. Only when her head began to droop did he lead them beneath the nearest dock. Wyatt curled up behind her with his head resting on her side, where he watched the sun rise until they drifted off to sleep.

## 13

Sky woke to a cold nose nudging her shoulder. Her eyes snapped open to the sound of the ocean nearby. A pure black wolf towered over her, his mouth quirked in an odd grin. Wyatt nudged her again, and she scrambled to her feet. He gestured toward the hotel and she nodded, yipping when his teeth closed around her ear. He stood before her, his eyes alive with mischief.

Understanding lit within her, and Sky dropped low, wriggling her rear. He wanted to race back, and she was ready. Last night he'd won by a landslide, but this morning, her wolf felt the need to kick a little ass.

He barked once, then twice...Sky shot forward, refusing to wait for the third bark. She heard his snarl behind her, and she huffed as she wound through the streets, nails gripping the pavement.

Running through the streets as wolves was hardly the most intelligent thing they could have done, but Sky loved it. She hadn't felt so free or alive in years. She hadn't realized how lonely her life had been.

A block before the hotel, Wyatt released a burst of speed and tore in front of her. Growling, she took the first left, a short cut she'd learned as a teenager. Her ears twitched as she listened to him scramble to catch up. Her legs felt like rubber, but she pushed harder and then launched into the air and clawed her way up the stairwell they'd descended the night before.

With a gleeful bark, she dove through the open window and shifted back to her human form. She'd won! She couldn't believe it! A rush of pleasure punched through her stomach as she staggered to her feet. She turned with a grin, her heart taking wing at the sight of Wyatt stalking toward her. Desire burned in his eyes, his jaw a hard line.

"You cheated."

"I did not." She laughed as she stepped backward. "But I do know all the shortcuts."

He came up flush against her, his amber gaze raking over her nude length. Without warning, his mouth came down on hers, and it was like *fire*, blazing through her entire body. *Hell*, the man could kiss. He ravaged her mouth with the same ferocity he did with everything else. Impatient and eager, Sky slid her fingers through his hair and held on for dear life as he shoved her against the wall and ground his hips against her.

Breaking from the kiss, he dragged his lips down the length of her neck and set his teeth against her throat, the slight pressure a silent question. She knew what he wanted, felt it in the hard scrape of his teeth. Sky's heart

Reach for the Sky

gave a hard kick, her stomach twisting with mindless desire. The need to let him claim her was so strong, her wolf's demand impossible to deny.

*It would be forever.*

But her wolf snarled, as though offended by the warning.

Would it be so bad? To surrender to her desires? She'd sworn to herself that she would never allow any man to do to her what her former alpha had done to her pack. But this was different. She was an adult now, capable of standing up for herself, as she'd proven more than once.

Becoming his…she toyed with the idea, her body lighting up as she envisioned them together. If she was being honest, the idea of becoming Wyatt Turner's mate was intoxicating.

His teeth sank a little deeper, reminding her of his presence. With a stifled gasp, her knees went boneless. She sunk into his embrace, a dark demand in the back of her mind begging she let him do this. Her wolf prowled the shadowed recess, yipping anxiously as though this was the moment she'd been waiting for.

"Sky," he whispered against her neck, his fingers digging into her side. He drew back, golden eyes blazing and chest heaving as he studied her. "Give me this."

Summoning her strength, she slipped her arms around his neck and leaned in, teeth catching his ear lobe. "Is that really how you ask a woman to be your mate?"

His chest vibrated against hers, his growl rumbling against her neck. "I've never asked anyone to be my mate before."

Her hands ran down his length, nails digging into his back. Wyatt shivered against her, his head dropping into the crook of her shoulder. "Well, there should be flowers, and chocolate, and you should be down on one knee—"

"In case you haven't noticed, I'm not exactly a flowers and candy sort of guy," he muttered as his hands slid under her rear and pulled her flush against him. "Definitely not the down on one knee sort either."

Sky poked out her bottom lip, her playful nature taking hold. "But it shouldn't be all about you."

"Mm." He dragged his chilled nose down her collarbone, his tongue laving at her skin. "It shouldn't be all about you either."

"All right." Her breath hitched when his mouth latched around her nipple. "Matching tattoos."

He chuckled, his teeth scraping against her as he glanced up. "You want matching tattoos?"

"You don't?" She lifted a teasing brow, her mouth parting when he gripped her waist and lifted, resting her knees against his hips. Braced against the wall, her head fell back when he dipped a finger within her, pumping as eagerly as she was against him. "I thought..." she moaned, her eyes crossing when his thumb came down on her clit, "...you'd like that idea."

"Keep talking," he whispered in a hoarse voice as he added a second finger.

She groaned, fingers latched in his hair as he bent over and worked his way to her pebbled nipples. "Matching motorcycles?" Not that either of them were actually thinking about it, not with his fingers fucking her against the wall. Warmth pooled in her belly and her toes curled. She cried out, about to shatter around his digits when Wyatt slowed his pace.

He straightened and took her mouth, swallowing her desperate moan. Sky pressed her bare breasts against his chest and rocked against him. With Wyatt, it would always be this intense heat and desire. And the thought excited her like nothing else. She'd suffered through enough monotony in her life with her former pack. This was what she wanted, this passion that burned them from the inside out.

He drew back, his reddened lips and half-lidded eyes tightening her gut. "You want a motorcycle?" As though he only now realized what she'd suggested.

She shook her head and stole another kiss, praying that he touched her again. Her body cried out for him to fill it, her stomach tight with need. "I don't know," she whispered raggedly against him. "Maybe. Could be fun."

He grunted, then turned, and pushed her against the opposite wall. "Is that a yes, then?"

"I don't know...are you going to buy me a motorcycle?"

With a soft snarl, he swept her over to the bed. "Darling, I'll buy you whatever you want." He dropped her down onto the mattress, waiting for her to settle against it before he knelt on the bed and prowled toward her with eyes as hard as his cock. "Say yes, Sky."

"I'm sorry, to what are you referring? I don't recall a question."

He growled, then gripped her thighs and eased them apart. Sky gasped as he lowered himself between her legs and drew his hot tongue over her sex. "Say yes," he muttered against her.

She felt him coming apart, knew that he was dying for her answer as to whether or not she would be his mate, but she found herself enjoying this little game. There was no longer any doubt in her mind; her answer would be yes, but part of her wanted him to beg, wanted to see such a dominant male brought down by a female.

His tongue teased her entrance, the golden gaze of his wolf watching her from between her thighs. *Holy hell...* she choked on her next breath when he grazed his newly-sprouted fangs against her clit. Her back shot off the bed, her fingers gripping the bedspread. Heat pooled in her stomach, the same orgasm from before rearing its head once again. She shuddered as she fell back, her glazed eyes blinking up at the ceiling.

"Skylar..."

His mouth sealed around her clit, his tongue working her until her breath came fast and hard. Her limbs tingled, her breasts heavy and aching to be touched. As though to emphasize his point, he slid his two fingers home, working her from inside and out. Sky cried out, desire eliciting a stronger reaction than she was accustomed to.

*Close*...her breath rushed past her lips, and her body hovered on that sweet precipice. A lick, a nip...the smallest touch would have shoved her over the edge. Instead, Wyatt pulled back, his amber eyes snapping open to watch her once more. "Sky, tell me what you want."

*Finally*...she dropped her head back against the

pillow with a frustrated cry. "You," she whimpered, hopelessly desperate to come.

He climbed her length, licking and nibbling his way to her mouth. Their tongues met in a frenzied tangle, and for the first time, she wrapped her hand around his erection. Wyatt moaned into her mouth, his hips thrusting as she stroked him. What she wanted was to feel him between her lips, taste his excitement in the back of her throat. Palm against his chest, she flipped him over and gazed down on him.

Desire darkened his eyes, but it was his swollen length that called her attention. "Sky, I need to know."

It was a dangerous game she was playing, and her keyed-up body demanded a release—the same release he continued to deny her as he awaited her answer. Seemed the alpha had found his own way of driving her to the brink.

Desperate to satisfy her wolf, she leaned down and kissed him again, working her tongue and hand together.

"Yes," she finally whispered as she slid down his body.

Her mouth actually ached for his cock. And she knew from the quiver in Wyatt's stomach as she tongued her way down that he would relish it too.

Grasping his cock, she licked his tip, reveling in the taste before she slid her mouth down his steeled length. Wyatt shot up from the bed, his hands gripping her arms and flipping their positions. "Damn it, Sky." He shook his head, his eyes a bit frantic as he batted her hand away from him. "I'm serious about this. This is it. This is what you get. Me. I've never been anything but honest with you about who I am. Be sure before you say yes."

She'd flipped the switch. There was no going back now. She'd agreed to mate with Wyatt, and the triumphant gleam in his eyes stunned her. She hadn't realized how badly he wanted her.

Still panting for air, Wyatt gazed down on her. "You need to be sure."

Nerves trilled deep in her stomach. Living among humans had revealed their need to court for years before offering such a pledge. Werewolves knew. Whether it was biological or psychological, she had yet to put her finger on it. However, *knowing* didn't guarantee a happily-ever-after. Her own parents were evidence of that.

Still, she couldn't escape the need to mate with him. Her wolf would never let her walk away, and as she stared up at him, she realized she didn't want to.

"Yes." Her voice was resolute this time, her decision made.

"Yes," he repeated.

She nodded. "Now, can I taste your cock?"

His eyes shuttered at her words, but rather than relinquish control, he settled himself between her thighs and thrust himself past her damp entrance.

---

Wyatt wanted to howl with satisfaction. Not only had she agreed to be his mate, but now he was sheathed within her, all wet and tight. Groaning, he dropped his head forward as he withdrew slowly and then glided back in. He'd meant to take it slow their first time together, show her exactly what he could do for her. But the woman was scorching. She stole his control and turned him into some mindless beast that wanted to fuck her senseless.

"Wyatt, please," she whimpered, her nails digging into his ass as she begged him to move.

*Fuck it.* He wrapped her legs around his waist and started thrusting, mesmerized by the expressions that flickered across her face. Mouth parted, her head deepened into the pillows, and she cried his name. Victory urged him faster until he lost all rhythm. Sky moaned, her fingers digging into his back as her entire body shattered around him. He couldn't look away as pure rapture spread over her face, her lashes fluttering against her cheeks as she rode out her orgasm.

He was close, felt the pleasure snaking down his body, felt his balls swell and his cock thicken within her. And while he wanted nothing more than to follow in her wake, he wasn't ready.

Instead, he gripped her thighs and flipped them over so that she straddled him from above.

"When I say the word, lean over me and bare your throat."

She swallowed and nodded before she started to move over him. Wyatt had intended to fuck her from beneath, make her come again, but he couldn't force himself to move, his eyes riveted to the sight of her riding him. *Boy howdy...* Her breasts shifted with her graceful movements, her head thrown back as she pleasured herself on his cock.

"Sky..." His ragged voice brought her gaze down on him, half-lidded and deeply blue. Then her mouth quirked into a devilish grin and his heart stuttered. She would be the death of him, of that he had no doubt. But there were worse ways to go.

She leaned back and placed her palms against his thighs, her hips thrust forward. This time when she moved, it was harder and quicker, her pace erratic. Wyatt's breath caught in his throat, his fingers gripping her legs as his eyes rolled back. *Christ*...he groaned, heat spreading through his cock when she came for a second time.

"Now," he growled.

She dropped over him and bared her neck. His canines ached, but rather than sink them into her throat, he gripped her ass and lifted her in the air, slamming into her over and over. Her cries were music to his ears, and when he felt his own orgasm plow through him, he buried his fangs right above her jugular.

*Bliss*...it was the only word he could think of as magic crashed into them and they cried out together, the pleasure cresting within him until he felt his body tremble from the most intense orgasm he'd ever experienced.

A fluttered breath brushed against his throat as Sky's weight settled on top of him. Without thought, Wyatt's arms curved around her, holding her close. This was new for him. In his experience, once he finished, he was out the door as fast as possible.

But this was his *mate*.

He blinked and stared up at the ceiling. His mate. He threaded his fingers through her beautiful hair and gazed into her face. Her eyes were closed and a small smile curved her lips.

Did he regret what they'd done?

He pushed her hair behind her ear and placed a gentle kiss against her brow.

Not on his fucking life.

# 14

---

S ky snorted herself awake, eyes snapping open at that intrusive sound. *Ugh,* she'd always hated that about Hidden Creek. They kept the rooms cold and dry to combat the humidity that awaited them outside. Clearing her throat, she wiped the sleep from her eyes and stretched, seeking Wyatt. Instead, her fingers found a crisp paper swan tucked against his pillow.

Chuckling, she held up the swan and carefully unfolded it. *Breakfast, be back soon.* Her mouth tugged and she spent the next ten minutes attempting to refold the note. *How the hell...* Exasperated, she tossed it back down onto the bed and stretched once more. Every muscle in her body ached, but it was a pleasant ache that reminded her of last night. Wyatt had proven himself insatiable, not that she'd complained. It wasn't as though she'd experimented with many human men in the past ten years. Though she loathed her old pack, she didn't loathe her wolf, nor did she revel in hiding half of herself from any lover. And after the humans had learned of her kind, those interested in sleeping with a werewolf weren't the sort she was interested in.

The hotel door swung open, and Wyatt strode in, a massive tray of food balanced in his palm.

"What did you do?" She laughed. "Rob the kitchen?"

He shot her a wolfish grin. "As a matter of fact..."

"What are you waiting for?" She wriggled her eyebrows. "Bring me some food! I'm starved."

He leaned over the bed and kissed her, the platter of food balanced perfectly above their heads. "Mm, me too. And not just for food."

Teasing, Sky reached for the plate. "I just want food."

Wyatt straightened, his free hand clutched over his chest. "My poor heart." He flashed her a stunning grin and reached for a bagel. "Now, you get nothing."

Sky blinked as he took a large bite of bagel. Their adventures had only ended a few hours ago, and her stomach begged for sustenance. "Wyatt..." she growled. Clutching the sheets to her chest, she rose from the bed and reached for the luscious selection of strawberries.

"Ah, ah." He waggled a finger at her and lifted the plate high above his head. "Mean wolves don't get fruit."

"What?" Her mouth dropped as she raked a starving glance over the assorted goodies.

"As alpha, I can't reward such mean behavior. Now, tell me you want my body and you can eat."

Sky burst out laughing. "Oh, so that's how this is?"

"Mhmm."

She unleashed her worst growl and stepped up flush to him, her fingers loosening on the sheet.

"Oh, so fierce," he teased, steel eyes sparking with a challenge. "What are you going to do? Growl me to death?"

She leapt into the air and snatched at the plate, her fingers grazing the ceramic before he spun out of reach.

"Too slow!" He laughed as he popped a plump cherry in his mouth. "Come on, Sky. I'm almost full and you haven't gotten a single bite yet. Say you're sorry and the whole plate is yours."

"And if I refuse?" she challenged with a playful glare.

"Ah, then alas, no breakfast for you."

"*Alas*?" She laughed.

"Hey! I read! Would you prefer I'd said, 'then you'd be shit out of luck'?"

"Maybe." She couldn't help the smile that spread across her face.

"That's two insults this morning." He flicked up two fingers and tsked at her. "And after all I did for you last night."

"Did for *me*?"

He laughed. "Please. Like you'd make the effort to get yourself off *that* many times."

A furious blush scoured her cheeks.

"Better hurry up and apologize, Sky. Otherwise I'm going to eat this entire plate..."

Two could play at that game. She released the sheet and watched mischievously as the material pooled around her feet. Wyatt's laughter died on a sharp breath. With a low hum, she eased down onto the bed, then stretched upward with her arms, displaying every curve. She braved a glance, her heart pattering at the sight of a far more primal hunger awakening within him.

*Like taking candy from a baby...*

Appealing to his alpha nature, she poked out her bottom lip. "But I'm so hungry. I need something warm and solid to fill me..."

His Adam's apple tensed as he swallowed. Dominant or not, she still had a trick or two up her sleeve. She locked her feet around his ass and drew him toward the bed while running her fingertips across her marked throat. "Don't you wanna fill me up, Wyatt?" She purred his name, then reached for the lip of his pants.

"*Christ*, Sky..."

The plate toppled to the bed and fruit spilled over the sheets, forgotten. Wyatt leaned over and stole a scorching kiss. Part of her recognized the win, but his lips had evoked a different hunger in her as well, one that pushed all other thoughts aside.

Breakfast? She didn't need no stinkin' breakfast.

---

Trapped together between the sheets, Wyatt winced as Sky snatched a plump raspberry from between his fingers. "Ow! Jesus, woman." He grunted, and admonished her with a quick tap on the nose. "Watch the teeth or no more playtime for you."

A sly grin curled her mouth. They'd already gone down that road, twice in fact. Who knew fruit could be so much fun in bed? She snatched at another berry, her teeth grazing him once more, when a resounding knock on the door sent her into a scramble.

Wyatt cursed, his breath catching when her knee grazed a rather sensitive area. "Easy, there."

As she reached for her clothes, Wyatt hopped into his jeans and started for the door. There had better be a damned good reason why someone was interrupting them. He rounded the bed and gestured for Sky to move to the far side of the room. "Let me see who it is first." He wasn't taking any chances.

Neither was given the chance. Instead, the door crashed open to reveal a tall, slightly older man. Both men froze, one on either side of the doorway. Wyatt drew in a deep breath, the scent of werewolf clouding his nose.

Snarling, he lunged forward and grabbed the intruder by his throat, slamming him into the nearest wall.

"Who the fuck are you? And don't you know how to knock?" He stole a glance back at Sky, relieved to see her dressed. She was scrambling with her shoes, her frightened eyes peering through a curtain of mussed hair.

The unwelcome werewolf crooked a brow and swept a dismissive glance down Wyatt's length. "I did. You took too long to open the door."

Wyatt slammed the guy against the wall once more for good measure. "Who are you?"

"Wyatt!" Sky cried out as she ducked around him.

People were gathering in the hallway, their mouths gaping as they watched the scene unfold. Wyatt didn't give a shit about civilians. Sky was his primary concern, and there was no way in hell he would allow some strange werewolf to wander into their room.

Her fingers dug into his forearm. "Wyatt, stop!"

"Better get your mate under control, girl," the intruder grumbled, "before I show him how a real alpha handles things."

Anger flared under his skin, and with a snarl, Wyatt shook him like a dog. "I'd watch myself if I were you."

"You abusive like this with all your wolves?" Hardened cobalt eyes stared up at him, his mouth a twisted sneer. "Sky would be better off with someone else."

Wyatt gnashed his teeth. "Maybe you would be better off telling me who you are before I rip out your throat on principle."

"Stop it!" Sky shoved him, but he hardly budged.

"Someone better start talking," he growled.

"Ease up!" she hissed. "He's my alpha. Well, former alpha."

"And grandfather," the werewolf snarled, flashing his lengthened canines.

Wyatt leaned forward and met the growl with one of his own.

"Oh, my God!" Sky shouted. "I am so sick of this male bullshit!"

Wyatt startled, his eyes widening at the sound of Sky cursing. It sounded so unnatural coming from her lips, and when he caught a glimpse of her, he found her pacing the length of the room, her face flushed and her eyes aglow. For the sake of his mate, Wyatt shoved away from her grandfather and crossed the room. "Alpha or not, you had no right to barge into our room like that."

"I have *every* right. Or don't you understand the

concept of territory? You're standing in *mine*, not the other way around. You breached my domain last night without a courtesy call. Be grateful I'm granting you this audience. I have every right to flay your hide, boy. So curb your tongue."

"Enough!" Sky stomped between them and slapped her hands flush against their chests. "Grandpa, we didn't come here to start some stupid war."

"Then why did you come?" His chilled gazed rooted on Sky, his mouth a grim line.

At a loss for words, Sky dropped her hand from her grandfather, but left the other pressed against Wyatt's chest. Tempting the fates, Wyatt reached up and twined their fingers together.

"Sky is in danger," Wyatt spoke, his voice shivering with rage. He hadn't known her grandfather was the alpha of the local pack, not that it changed anything.

The guy was older than the average alpha, but from the steeled frame and hardened muscles, it was easy to see how he'd maintained his position. His salt-and-pepper hair was the only thing that betrayed his age.

"And? What? Not dominant enough to handle it yourself?"

Wyatt tensed. "Listen, old man—"

"Stop it," Sky hissed. "Wyatt, maybe you should step out for a bit and let me speak with my grandfather."

"Not on your life," he grumbled.

Sighing, Sky's head dropped forward, and she massaged her temples. There was a part of him that regretted upsetting her, but the other, more dominant part, refused to leave her alone in any man's company other than his. And that had nothing to do with his claim on her and everything to do with her safety.

"Wyatt...please. My grandfather isn't going to harm me."

His jaw ticked. "Seems to me he already has."

And wasn't that the truth. He hadn't forgotten what Sky had divulged. Her aspirations for a career and a life beyond a begrudged mating had earned her a one-way exile from the pack. Though she'd never admit it aloud, he could see how it had affected her. Rejection in any form had lasting effects.

"Listen here, you little punk..."

Wyatt sized the man up, his muscles coiling in preparation for an attack.

"I can't handle this much testosterone," Sky whispered. "Grandpa, follow me."

Without another word, she grasped her grandfather's hand and led him toward the door. Only then did she toss a glance over her shoulder and shake her head at Wyatt, subtly informing him to stay behind.

The door clicked behind them, and cursing, Wyatt stalked toward the open window. Like hell he was going to sit in the hotel room and wait for them to return.

Leaping down the eight floors, he stalked toward the hotel lobby, his head turning at the sound of a sharp gasp. The hotel receptionist from last night stopped dead in her tracks, a half-eaten sandwich dangling from her fingertips. Fear perfumed the air as Wyatt strode by. Well, if she hadn't known they were werewolves before, she likely did now.

At the entrance, he stopped and poked his head

around the corner. Sure enough, Sky sat in the lobby with her grandfather, her head braced between her hands. Though he wanted nothing more than to stand next to her during this ordeal, he knew her grandfather would never reveal anything with him present. So, he swallowed his pride and hung back. If this meeting garnered any information, it would be worth it.

## 15

Sky nudged open the hotel room door and entered with a long sigh. Wyatt's rich scent welcomed her, and when she lifted her head, it was to find him standing next to the bed, exactly where she'd left him. Rolling her eyes, she scooted past him and slumped into the nearby chair. If he thought she hadn't seen him down there, he had another thing coming. She'd never admit it, but she appreciated that he'd done that much for her. It was difficult for an alpha werewolf to leave someone they considered weaker exposed and vulnerable.

"Well?" he murmured, crouching in front of her.

Sky's gaze raked over his hardened face. Beneath the rough exterior and excess testosterone, there was an honest man. She reached out and caressed his scar with the pad of her thumb. "How did this happen?"

His mouth quirked, tugging the scar across his face. "You want to talk about my scars?"

She studied the one above his eye and smoothed his

brow. "Humor me." She needed a moment to digest her visit with her grandfather.

"All right." He grasped her hand and drew it toward his mouth, running her fingers along his lips. "Before I became an alpha, I was a no-account mechanic. I bled oil."

"That explains *Monster*," she said with a small smile.

He nodded. "Before I took the alpha position, I was easily bored. So...whenever that happened, I ventured downtown and found a way to entertain myself."

Fear clawed at Sky's stomach. What the heck did that even mean? Was he referring to prostitutes? And what did that have to do with his scars?

His chuckle cleared her thoughts. "It's not as bad as you're thinking, I assure you. I'd enter into the underground fighting rings."

Her mouth dropped. "You...gambled with your life?" How was that not as bad?

He shrugged. "It was something to do. I knew my limits. Some nights I got my ass handed to me, and others I won."

"Did they know you were a werewolf?"

A deep chuckle vibrated against her hand. He kissed her palm and then lowered it. "Of course they did. It was a werewolf fighting ring. No rules, no weapons. Just you and your wolf form. It's how I became an alpha. The fights forced me to control my wolf."

"Control your wolf." She snickered. "I haven't witnessed any of this control you speak of."

Wyatt cleared his throat and met her gaze. "Ya, well,

you sort of undo me." He squared his shoulders as though daring her to tease him. "Happy?"

Speechless, Sky leaned forward and brushed her mouth across his. A chaste kiss, but one filled with emotion. "That doesn't explain the scars."

"Ah. Well, let me save you those gory details. Essentially, someone got the upper hand, literally."

She nodded. Werewolves were fast healers, but wounds caused by other werewolves healed human-slow. "So, underground fighting, hey?"

Wyatt lifted a brow. "Don't tell me that turns you on?"

"No!" She laughed. "I didn't see you as the sort."

"Really. You didn't see *me* as the sort to get down and dirty and bloody?"

Her mouth twitched. "Well, when you put it that way..."

"So now that I've told you mine, are you going to tell me what went down with your grandfather?"

She grimaced and leaned back in the chair.

---

Wyatt watched as Sky draped herself in the chair, clearly dreading this conversation. Finally, she blinked and met his gaze. "I told my grandfather what was happening. He was appalled."

There was a flash of something behind her eyes, a dark emotion that Wyatt read as easily as he did a book. "But he blames me."

Her gaze flitted away. "He said that as an alpha, it's your responsibility to put a stop to this."

Though the insult burned, Wyatt didn't disagree. The old man was right about something, at least. And it was something that he was trying to make right. "Anything else, other than insulting my competence?"

"Unfortunately, no. All his wolves are accounted for. Which means none of them have been off murdering or blinding women in Colorado."

Cursing, Wyatt leaned back on his haunches and gazed out the window. Well, their best lead had fizzled. And yet, it'd made so much sense. None of this had happened before her mother's death, before Sky had returned to the pack for the funeral.

"Was there anyone else at the funeral that you can think of? Anyone that wasn't of your pack? Anyone that stood out?"

She nibbled her bottom lip, her brows knotting. "Not that I can remember. It was a year ago, Wyatt. And I wasn't exactly in the state of mind to notice who was there."

He sighed and dropped onto the floor. Eyes focused on the ceiling, he played through the events that Sky had listed once more. "You said your mother and you hadn't spoken in over a decade. Why?"

"It doesn't matter—"

"At this point, I'm not ruling anything out. So, why?"

Sky groaned and dropped her hands down the side of the chair. "My mother thought I'd acted rashly. She thought I'd turned away from the pack and my family by choosing a career instead. When I left, she told me not to expect to be welcomed back. I went to school anyway. I thought once they saw what I was doing, they'd understand."

"But they didn't," Wyatt stated.

"No. I graduated and my grandfather contacted me. He told me it was time to come home. I had *responsibilities*." She scoffed. "Right. What he meant was it was time for me to choose a mate and pump out babies. I disobeyed his order and, instead, applied for grad school."

Wyatt's brows shot up. "Your grandfather actually expected you to come home just to have children?"

Sky sneered. "It's their way, something I've always loathed. My grandfather believes a woman's first and foremost responsibility is to take care of the pack. And when she isn't pregnant, she's a homemaker or caregiver. My grandfather is old-fashioned, and he pushed those stupid beliefs onto the pack."

Wyatt shook his head. Old-fashioned was right. He encouraged the females in his pack to broaden their horizons. Travel, education, career, anything that could help strengthen the pack. If they chose to mate and have children, it was their choice—he would never force them.

"When I finished my master's, my grandfather contacted me once more. He claimed that he'd been generous, and that he'd given me my freedom for long enough. This time, he sent two of the males, my brother included, to fetch me. Their orders were to bring me home, no discussion."

"But you didn't return."

A bitter chuckle scraped past her lips. "No, I sent

Sawyer packing with a black eye and a broken rib. He'd given me a few good knocks, but hardly enough to win." She smiled wistfully. "My brother hasn't won a scrap against me since we were teenagers, but I suspect that has more to do with his upbringing than anything. My grandfather believed men were meant to protect women, not hit them. And thank goodness for that. He might have knocked me out cold and dragged me home, otherwise."

Wyatt grinned and tucked his hands under his head. "Can't imagine your grandfather appreciated that."

"Not at all. He phoned and I told him to stuff his rules where the sun don't shine. Told him I'd begun my doctorate and there was no way in hell I was coming home."

"And then he exiled you."

Her silence was answer enough.

"And this led to your mother rejecting you?"

He heard her swallow. "My mother and I had always been on shaky ground. I disagreed with my parents' marriage. Felt that they weren't suited for one another, and that my mother should have left. She disagreed, said she had a good life. My father screwed anything on two legs. How was that a good life? Again, it boiled down to her upbringing. They had mated one another, and there was no way to break that, so why bother changing anything? Eventually, my father grew tired of my mother and left. Neither could choose new mates, but my mother did remarry. There were times when I thought her new husband, Landon, might be her true mate, but there was nothing they could do about it.

She had his children, but wasn't able to solidify their bond."

*Ah...*Wyatt nodded as he stared up at the ceiling. This explained so much about Sky and her resistance to authority. It was a wonder he'd convinced her to mate with him.

"When I left, my mother told me not to come back. I'd thought that once I was awarded my doctorate, they would understand and accept me back. But she died before that could happen."

"You're still working toward it?"

She shifted in her seat. "Have been for the past three years. It's a brand new field and all new research, so it'll take longer than the average doctorate."

"New field, as in something regarding werewolves?"

She nodded. "And their ability to blend in with human society."

Wyatt's head lolled against the floor. She sat in the chair, her eyes closed as she spoke. She seemed so peaceful, a sight he rather liked.

"I tried tracing our lineage back to the first werewolf." She gave a little shake of her head. "Bunked out. Too many legends. But I know that we've been around for millennia. There's literature for Native American origins, European origins...it's all so murky. However, our ability to blend among humans is renowned. Werewolves never reveal themselves until they kill. It's quite an adaptive ability."

Wyatt's head started to spin. "All right, so what does that have to do with anything?"

She chuckled and pinned him with a playful stare. "It

has to do with *everything*. We possess an innate ability to suppress our wolves. Look how you reacted to my grandfather when he barged in. Out came your wolf and you two were slathering at each other, hoping to rip each other a new hole. Had he been a human, you would have pushed your wolf back and controlled it. For all intents and purposes, you would have acted human. Studies have proven that some alpha werewolves possess the ability to mask their scents, to hide in plain sight of those they deem a threat. It's fascinating."

Wyatt hummed a vague response.

"My theory is that this ability has caused *instability* within some wolves. Suppressing their inner nature results in an unbalanced psyche, which can result in deviant behavior."

"All right, all right," Wyatt laughed. "I get it. You're passionate about this."

"Yes. Something my grandfather never recognized. Anyway, understanding werewolf behavior, psychology, and evolution could help the humans accept us."

He felt a surge of pride for his mate. He had to admit, if anyone could breach the gap between the two species, it was her. She was the perfect candidate both physically and intellectually. Who better to be the public face of werewolves than a lean, blonde, and blue-eyed girl? Unfortunately, her looks were likely what had attracted the attention of her stalker.

"My grandfather has invited us to a feast tonight," she mumbled after a few moments of silence.

Wyatt glanced at her, his brows twisting. "What?"

*No.* Their obligations back home had to take precedence. Bale had done well enough, but the pack wasn't safe.

"I don't understand it either. First, they exiled me, and now they want to throw a party in my honor. I can't imagine that's sitting well with the other females. I'm a pariah to them."

*Oh*, Wyatt understood. A game of dominance and politics among alphas. The old man wanted him to know that Sky was theirs, regardless of her exile.

"No." He shook his head. "We're heading back to Colorado immediately."

"Normally, I would agree with you..."

"But?" Of course she had to argue.

Sighing, Sky leaned forward in the chair. "It isn't every day I get to see my family under welcoming circumstances. Not to mention..." She blushed. "I want to show them what they're missing out on."

A fierce surge to protect her welled within him. "You want to rub their noses in what you've become."

"Is that so bad?" Her mouth grimaced. "I'm a horrible person, aren't I?"

He laughed and rocked to his feet. "Nah, it's justified." Then, with a grim expression, he grasped her hands and drew her to her feet. "But in all seriousness, I'd rather we head home."

"Wyatt. One more night, that's all I'm asking."

"All right," he sighed. "How is it that you get me to do everything *you* want?"

"Just lucky, I suppose."

## 16

"That's my mother's cabin, right over that small hill." Sky leaned against the car door and gazed across the land as their chauffeur, Gordon Hall, drove them to her grandfather's, her thoughts plummeting to a dark place.

Someone had been maintaining it in her mother's stead. After the funeral—and after her grandfather had unceremoniously demanded that she leave—she'd stopped at the small cabin and spent the night among her mother's possessions. Though her mother hadn't used it since remarrying, it was still a part of her.

No matter that the later years had been rife with anger and frustration, Sky knew that her mother had once loved her. So, that night, she'd curled up on the bed, pulled her mother's blankets close, and wept for the future they would never have.

"This is hard for you." There was no question in Wyatt's soft voice.

"The last time I was here, it was to say goodbye to someone I once loved. I felt such guilt when I arrived. If only I'd tried to mend things, or made an effort to reach out. But when they shunned me, I was so angry. They were my pack. They were supposed to love me no matter what choices I made with *my* life. Everything was always about *them*, though. They wanted me to fall in line, pump out babies...live a life I never wanted."

Wyatt brought her hand to his mouth and brushed his lips against her knuckles. Her heart fluttered, a small smile touching her lips. Away from his pack, there was a marked difference in him. Gone was the alpha attitude that often irritated her. Left in its stead was *Wyatt*—someone she knew she could love. Sometimes, the wolf chose the mate and left the human half to catch up, and sometimes, the human half never caught up, as evidenced by her parents. How her father had silenced his wolf long enough to screw around was something she'd never understood. Nor did it matter any longer. He lived on the east coast—she'd never bothered to ask where—and her mother was dead.

The soft whirr of the partition lowering broke the silence. "We're almost there."

Sky glanced up and nodded, meeting Hall's gaze in the rear-view mirror. Her grandfather had sent a vehicle for them, which had rankled Wyatt to no end. She'd kept him occupied, though, telling tales of her family along the way.

She smoothed her hands down her outfit, her stomach twisting. Neither Sky nor Wyatt had packed for this, and they'd been given no time to shop before the gathering. Thankfully, she'd brought an extra tank top, which she'd covered with Wyatt's leather jacket. It swallowed her lithe frame, but his scent helped calm her.

Hall pulled up to the house and into the driveway. Without waiting, she popped open the backdoor and hopped out. Much like the rest of Hidden Creek, her grandfather's house hadn't changed in her time away.

"This way." Hall gestured toward the entry.

Sky and Wyatt shared a glance before they walked up the path and slipped through the door. The estate was a little larger than Wyatt's, and far removed from the public. It was the vision her grandfather had always aspired to.

"Skylar!" Her name echoed through the gilded hallway.

She lifted her chin and sought out the source. There, at the end of the corridor, was her sister-in-law, Amberly. Sky had been fifteen when her older brother had announced his mating. At eighteen, she had felt he was far too young to commit himself to someone, but her family had been ecstatic that he had chosen someone. The startling realization that Sky *liked* Amberly had been jarring; she'd fully expected to loathe the woman who had forced herself into their family.

Amberly jogged down the hallway, her long skirt fluttering behind her. "Sky!" Then, with a giggle, she descended upon her and wrenched her into a hug. "When Sawyer heard you were coming..." She shook her head, tears glistening in her light brown eyes. "He's so excited to see you!"

Sky felt a natural smile curve her lips. Of her entire

family, Amberly had been the only one to show any support when she'd left. Not that it'd made a lick of difference. "Where is he?"

"Out with Paxton. There were a couple more things to pick up." She smiled fondly. "Oh, you should see Paxton! She's pregnant again!"

Sky blinked. Last she'd heard, Sawyer and Paxton hadn't been on speaking terms. Sawyer had never agreed with the way things had ended between their parents. And when their mother settled with her new mate, Landon, Sawyer had refused to acknowledge either of their resulting children.

"Things have changed in the past year," Amberly murmured. "Once your mother passed..." Her words trailed off until eventually she shrugged. "Sawyer sort of took Paxton and Noah under his wing. Landon isn't dealing well with the loss of your mother. He's getting better, but Noah needed someone to look up to."

And so he'd stepped up, something Sky hadn't been around for. Another surge of guilt washed through her.

"That's not important, though." Amberly threw a glance Wyatt's way before she leaned forward and whispered. "Maybe you could introduce us?"

"Oh!" Sky closed her eyes and shook her head. "Wyatt, this is my sister-in-law, Amberly. She's married to my brother, Sawyer."

"Pleasure to meet you." Amber offered a bright grin.

"And as I said, this is Wyatt, my...mate." Sure, she hesitated on the word, but who wouldn't after a mere twelve hours since the big event?

"Your...mate?" Amber brows shot up. "I didn't know

—I mean, no one told us. I thought, I mean we *all* thought—"

Sky's mouth tightened. "Thought what?"

An embarrassed blush scoured her sister-in-law's cheeks, and with a forced grin, she shook her head. "It doesn't matter. Wow, look how long we've been out here, we should...yes, I think they're ready for us. We should go."

"Wait." Skylar drew Amberly back with a hand on her arm. "What's going on?"

"Ignore me," she giggled. "Pregnancy hormones, and all that."

"You're pregnant too?" Sky's hand shot to her mouth and her eyes to Amberly's midsection.

"Six weeks. Confirmed yesterday." This time her grin was natural. "Now, come on, everyone is dying to see you."

"Doubtful," Sky grumbled as she followed in the wake of her bouncy sister-in-law. Wyatt's choked laugh caught her attention. "And what are you snickering about?"

Wyatt bit back a grin, his eyes twinkling with humor. "Sky, they thought you were gay."

The sudden proclamation brought her up short. "What?"

Laughter rolled from his lips. Alone in the hallway now, he slid his arms around her waist and drew her into his chest, his fingers sliding along the lip of her jeans. "She was legitimately shocked that you had taken a mate."

Annoyance settled in the pit of Sky's stomach. "You're joking."

"Nope." Wyatt choked back a fresh laugh. "Her face gave it away. She's probably rushing ahead to announce to everyone that you aren't a lesbian."

Groaning, Sky dropped her head onto Wyatt's chest. "Let's get this over with so we can go home."

He hooked a finger beneath her chin and lifted it. "To my place, right? Soon to be our place?"

"Is now really the time to have this conversation?"

He shrugged, then glanced around. "We're alone, why not? I can't imagine you'd want to return to your house."

Her house. Right. Where the bastard had slaughtered poor Jody Anne Davidson. "Let me get through this house first, all right?" So not to offend him, Sky rose up on her tiptoes and kissed him.

"As you wish," he murmured against her lips.

---

The cabin was dark, but ready.

For a year, he'd maintained it, and all for Skylar. He remembered the night of her mother's funeral well, had longed to go to her and dry her tears. She'd been alone and grieving and desperate for comfort, but the time hadn't been right.

Now, he was tired of waiting. Tired of others standing in his way. Tired of being denied that which was his. His nostrils flared, but Sky's scent had long since faded.

It hadn't taken long for sweet Trinity to divulge Sky's destination, and when he'd heard *Hidden Creek*, he'd felt a surge of pleasure like nothing else. Then, he'd cut out her eyes with a dreamy smile, content for the first time ever. And for once, he hadn't felt the need to slake his need, a reward reserved for Sky.

Though surrounded by her family, she was far more vulnerable here than in Wolffe Peak. Their eyes wouldn't track her twenty-four seven, nor was there a dedicated sheriff hounding her every step.

He turned and paced the length of the family room once more, feet wearing a new tread in the restored hardwood. So much effort had gone into the upkeep, and all for her, to make her feel welcome and loved and appreciated. After the miserable life her family had provided her, it was well-deserved. No other could provide her with that—no one else *understood* what those bastards had put her through. Oh, but he did. He knew the sting of exile as well as she did.

And once she was here, it was a sting they could ease...together.

He shivered with anticipation, his gaze landing upon the master bedroom. He strode toward it, his palms growing clammy as he gazed onto the bed. The restraints sat upon the mattress, the soft cuffs begging for her ankles and wrists. This was the place where he would show her how much he loved her, where he would bring her to the peak of pleasure, where he would hear her scream his name.

Only one person stood in his way.

His hand strayed to the small of his back, his fingers

touching the cold, steel gun pressed against him. One silver bullet was all it would take.

All he had to do was wait for his moment, and then Sky would be his forever.

## 17

Wyatt stood tall and watched those in attendance with great fascination. Seeing the inner workings of another pack was rare, but beyond that, he was watching for anything out of the ordinary. Though Sky's grandfather, Gavin, had deemed his pack innocent, it didn't necessarily mean it was true. Had another alpha come to Wyatt's pack to question the whereabouts of his people, he would have lied through his teeth and then investigated for himself.

Unfortunately, at this point, it seemed Gavin had spoken the truth. Though Sky had suffered some brutal questions and assumptions, few had shown interest in anything beyond her whereabouts for the past decade. Amberly had exaggerated their excitement to see her again; Sky had been quite right when she'd called herself a pariah.

"Walk with me," Gavin's voice sounded next to him.

Wyatt crooked his head and studied Sky's former

alpha. He settled against the wall, his burly arms crossed over his chest as though to appear intimidating. Wyatt snorted under his breath and shook his head. There was no doubt in his mind—if it came down to a fight, the old man didn't stand a chance. "No."

Gavin blinked. "Excuse me?"

For a moment, the corner of Wyatt's mouth twitched. The indignation in his voice was one that Sky mimicked perfectly.

"I wasn't asking."

Wyatt cocked a brow. He'd used that line himself a few times on Sky. He chuckled to himself and shook his head, marveling that she'd accepted him as her mate. Now he understood how she felt when he ordered her about. Hilarious how some things came full circle. "Good, because I'm not going anywhere with you. My job is to keep Sky safe. That means keeping an eye on her at all times."

"Sure, because that's the way to start off a new relationship, by smothering your mate."

"I'm not—"

"She's with her brothers. My boys will ensure no harm comes to her. You can spare a few moments to speak with your new mate's grandfather."

Wyatt spared a glance in her direction. The old wolf was correct—she was surrounded by a whole herd of family members. He scrubbed a warm hand down his face and sighed before following in Gavin's wake.

The old alpha led him to a small office, and once he stepped within, Gavin closed the door with a soft click.

"All right, get it all off your chest," Wyatt grumbled.

Gavin lifted his hard gaze. "I know what Sky has told you about us."

*All right, not how I expected this to start.* Wyatt frowned and slanted against the door, his legs crossed at the ankles. "Really."

"I would think, as an alpha, you would understand my perspective."

Wyatt gave a bitter chuckle. "Is that so?"

"I gave Sky multiple chances to return to us. Her constant rejection of my authority had begun to raise questions. I love my granddaughter with all my heart, but you should understand who it is that you've chosen as your mate. She disobeys every command, refuses to take her place in the hierarchy, and undermines all authority."

Wyatt's brows lifted. Her grandfather had listed every reason he loved her. Wyatt blinked, his loud thoughts drowning out Gavin. He hardly knew her, but he knew without a doubt he would do anything to have her in his life, forever. *I love her...* "Well, imagine that..."

Gavin's words trailed off, and he pinned Wyatt with an annoyed glare. "What?"

Wyatt shook his head. No need to pepper her grandfather with declarations of love. That was a little too...fruity for his liking. The only person he would ever utter those words to was Sky.

"Were you even listening to me?" Gavin sighed.

"Nah, not even a little bit. Did I miss anything important?"

The old man groaned. "Maybe you two are suited for each other. Must I threaten you? You will treat her well, right?"

"Like your threats would mean anything to me."

Wyatt pushed off the door and turned to leave, but before he did, a flash of something caught his eye. He hesitated, then reached out and plucked a titanium photo frame from the nearby bookshelf. The picture within was heartrending. Turning, he held it up, his fingers caressing the glass. "You keep photos of Sky?"

Gavin nodded, a pained expression twisting his face. "I told you, I love my granddaughter. This is my private study, so I keep her pictures here."

Wyatt lowered the photo and studied it. Draped in black, Sky stood next to an earthen mound, a single rose clutched to her chest as she stared down. The angle of the picture was just right to catch the single tear that scoured her cheek, and *boy howdy*, it was a knife to his heart. "Her mother's funeral?"

Gavin cleared his throat and nodded.

"You took a picture of her at her mother's funeral?"

"No." He sounded disgusted. "If you take the back off, you'll see it's a newspaper clipping. I've kept every article ever posted about her."

Wyatt lifted his head. "How many are there?"

"Quite a few."

"Show me."

Gavin's eyes narrowed. "Excuse me?"

Wyatt waved an impatient hand. There was something off about this photo, though he couldn't put his finger on it. What sort of reporter capitalized on someone's personal pain like this? He shook his head. All right, all of them, but this photo didn't sit well with him.

He studied it, his attention landing on the faint outline of bushes in the far edge of the picture.

"Here," Gavin grunted. "Knock yourself out."

Glancing up, Wyatt noted a box of trimmings, all stamped with Sky's image. "What the hell..." He reached for the box and pulled out the top two.

Sky at the presidential ball, following in line at her mother's funeral, standing behind a podium, coming out of the sheriff's office...it went on and on.

"Look at this," Wyatt muttered. He handed the picture frame to Gavin. "Down in the right corner. Does that look like an edge of a bush to you?"

"Ya, so?"

Wyatt sighed. "So, do you know many journalists who hide in the bushes to catch a snapshot? Gossip columnists, maybe, but these all belong to respected newspapers."

"So what?" Gavin dropped into his chair and nudged the box across the desk. "Sky welcomed this nonsense into her life when she took such a high profile job. These articles started the moment she completed her master's and entered into politics."

"Exactly," Wyatt murmured, his thoughts buzzing. This was an angle they hadn't approached yet. He'd thought it had something to do with her former pack, but maybe it didn't. Maybe the funeral had been the *trigger*. Something must have happened to instigate the stalking, but it didn't mean the stalker was someone local to Hidden Creek. "Who took all these photos?"

"I don't know." Gavin rocked back in his chair. "Never looked."

Flipping over the article, Wyatt's eyes widened at the familiar name. "*Son-of-a-bitch!*"

"What?"

He tore through the box, snatching out one article after another, finding the same name written on each of the images. *Mother fucker*, this obsession had been going on longer than they'd thought. *Years.* He sucked in a sharp breath and threw the articles back into the box. But how was it possible? He was human.

The answer had been given to him this afternoon in the hotel—Sky's thesis. "These are coming with me."

Gavin shot out of the chair. "What did you find?"

"I may be wrong, but I think I know who's stalking her."

"Who?"

Wyatt gestured toward the photos. It was the only logical explanation. "James Griffon, the journalist." He glanced up at Gavin. "I'm taking Sky home. This lead needs to be investigated."

Gavin gave a clipped nod. "Keep my girl safe."

For once, they agreed on something.

---

Sky sagged against the nearest wall and sighed, exhausted. She'd forgotten how tiring her family could be. Everything was always *who had mated with whom*, and *who was having a baby*. It all felt so superficial. She'd told Wyatt that she'd wanted to come back to rub her success in their faces, but not a single one of them cared about what she was working toward. Her brother had casually mentioned her career, but they'd simply nodded politely, as though it was of no interest to them.

After hearing Paxton talk about their upcoming fourth child—*two more months now!*—Sky had wandered off to find Wyatt, only to see him following her grandfather into his office. She couldn't imagine that was going to be a pleasant conversation, but she wasn't brave enough to interrupt.

Tipping her head back, she drew in another deep breath. Fresh air would be nice right about now...take a moment to stare at the moon and recharge her energy. She had the rest of the night to look forward to and already she was fading.

Pushing away from the wall, she made her way toward the front entrance and slipped on her boots. A few moments, that was all she needed.

"Sky?"

She lifted her head and peered through a curtain of hair to see Noah bearing down on her.

"Where are you going?" The teenager's face pinched, his brows knotted with concern.

Of all her half-siblings, Noah was by far her favorite. Paxton had only ever cared about dolls and hair, while Noah seemed more mature. Though he didn't yet understand the ways of the world, he seemed to care about them. She'd actually missed him when she'd left. "Out for a breath of fresh air."

"You shouldn't be alone right now." He glanced behind him. "Sawyer told me that someone is after you."

Fifteen, and already he carried the weight of the

world. With a gentle smile, she jerked her chin toward the door. "Care to join me? You can protect me."

The boy blushed, but after a sharp nod, he threw on his shoes and opened the door, his hand held out to keep Sky from leaving until he scented the air. Finally, he nodded. "All clear."

"You're going to make a fine man someday, kid."

His blush deepened. "I watch you on the news every chance I get."

It was a line she often heard, but from Noah, it was flattering. "Yeah?"

"I told Grandpa that I agreed with what you were doing."

She chuckled. "And how did that go over?"

The boy's mouth twisted. "I was assigned three weeks of landscape duty."

Ah, some things never changed. Sky blew out a breath, watching as it misted in the frosty air before being swept away by the chilled wind. Together, they walked across the property, the house shrinking in the distance. Pausing by the fence line, she stared at the moon, drawing on whatever energy she could. Out here, she felt free, the burdens of her family lifting from her shoulders. Home, she had Wyatt and his pack. Those who had accepted her without any hesitation. A smile had just cracked her lips when Noah gave a soft gasp.

Glancing his way, she frowned at the sight of his gaping mouth and twisted brows. "What is it, kid?"

His head dropped and she followed, blinking at the sight of a dark stain blooming across his chest. Dead center was a silver knife, gleaming in the moonlight.

"*Noah!*" Skylar shrieked, her hands reaching for him as a dark shadow rose behind him. Her brother sagged into her arms, his head lolling against her shoulder. Sky's gaze climbed the tall figure, her entire body going cold the moment she recognized him. "You..." Before she could suck in a breath, he descended upon her and something sharp pricked her neck.

The world tilted, and she staggered as her brother slipped from her grasp.

"Noah," she murmured, her boneless knees threatening to give out beneath her.

A savage snarl rent the night air, one that her mind instantly recognized. *Wyatt.* Her mouth shaped his name, but the only sound that escaped was a faint whimper.

James Griffon stood next to her, a wicked grin splitting his face as he lifted his arm. Steel glinted in his hand, and, with a gasp, Sky threw her weight at him. *Too slow!* Multiple gunshots rang in her head, and Sky's gaze snapped across the field where a monstrous wolf jerked mid-air and toppled to the ground.

*No!*

All she'd wanted was a breath of fresh air and to gaze up at the moon. She could see them now, twinkling up in the midnight sky. Her eyes grew heavy, and one-by-one, the stars winked out until nothing remained but darkness.

## 18

J ames brushed the back of his fingers down Skylar's smooth side. For years, he'd imagined this moment, but the fantasy had paled in comparison.

The moment he'd first laid eyes on her, he'd known. His sweet, sweet Sky. Nothing would keep them apart ever again. For years, he'd watched from the shadows, too intimidated to approach her in any fashion other than professional. So beautiful, so graceful, Skylar Callahan was out of his league. Every time he'd phoned, he'd failed to find the right words. He'd hoped his letters would clarify his feelings, but instead, they'd sent her into the arms of Shane. And so he'd waited for Sky to realize the sheriff wasn't right for her. Then came Wyatt... James gnashed his teeth as he thought of the fucking alpha. But now, Wyatt was no longer a threat, and finally, she was his.

He touched a lock of blonde hair and smoothed it back from her pale cheek. So beautiful. Her full lashes fluttered as though she might wake, but with a soft sigh, she settled deeper into sleep, the drugs carrying her further into her dreams. How he longed for her to wake, but the sedative had been necessary. He hadn't wanted to harm her, not like the others.

Lust lured him closer to her sleeping form, and with a shuddering breath, he inhaled the air around her. The drug's scent lingered, but with every passing moment, her sweet honeysuckle fragrance grew stronger. It wouldn't be long, now. A few hours, and then, *finally*, they would be together.

Gut quivering with anticipation, he stole a kiss from his Sleeping Beauty, reveling in the feel of her soft mouth. His heart thundered against his ribs, ratcheting his pulse until it deafened him. There'd never been a connection like this with any of the others. They'd been nothing more than substitutes, and poor ones at that. This...this was real. This was what he'd needed for so long.

Poised over her mouth, his hand crept up the length of her thigh, and his cock jumped. Excitement quickened his breath until he found himself panting above her. Consumed by his need, he slowly drew down his zipper and freed himself from his constraining jeans. *God*, he wanted nothing more than to sink himself within her, to take what he'd waited so long for. *Restraint*, he cautioned himself. Though his desire burned him from the inside out, he knew he had to wait for Sky to wake. Taking her in her sleep wouldn't sate his need. He wanted her awake, wanted her aware. He could only imagine the bliss when he rocked into her...he ground his jaw and sucked in a deep breath. Such thoughts wouldn't help chill his blood.

He pushed himself away from her. After craving her for so long, he never wanted them to be apart again. And with Wyatt dead, he would take her as his mate once she woke. He would plunge his fangs and cock into her, make her scream with rapture, and when he was done, she would be his.

He grunted and glanced down, noting the firm grip he held on himself. Excitement flushed his skin as his gaze strayed back to her. His breath hitched, his fully engorged cock throbbing for release. He'd already freed her from her clothes. Bare to the world, it would cost him nothing to bury himself between her legs and relieve the pressure.

*No...* He closed his eyes and gave himself a final squeeze, imagining Sky's fingers instead. He'd waited so long, what were a few more hours? The asshole was dead; the silver bullets to the chest had guaranteed that. All that remained was to mate with her, and then this whole ordeal would be finished.

With a strangled moan, he stuffed himself back into his pants and stretched out next to her, his fingers idly running across her stomach. He could wait.

And until then, he would watch.

———

Wyatt snarled, a mangled sound of pain and fury.

"Lie still!" Gavin barked. "You can't go stomping off

after her with a friggin' bullet inches from your heart and another in your gut."

"Hurry up!" he shouted.

His fingers flexed, a reaction to whatever the hell Gavin's people were doing to him. Searing pain scalded his chest, but it was nothing compared to the fear that had burrowed its way into his heart. *Sky*...she was out there, somewhere, and with James.

*James.*

How could he have been so blind? At every turn, the psychopath had been there, but he'd written off his persistence because he was a journalist. Wyatt dropped his head back against the kitchen table and growled. He'd ignored him because he'd thought he was human. But he'd sure scented him out in the fields—the bastard hadn't hidden himself well enough this time.

"Sit *still!*" Gavin yelled.

"Where would he have taken her?" He needed to focus on Sky, needed a plan to kill that son-of-a-bitch before he laid one goddamned finger on her.

Guilt perfumed the air. "I don't know," Gavin admitted. "Until we heard the gunshot, we didn't know anything was wrong. By the time we reached you, she was already gone."

Wyatt shoved Amberly's hands away from his chest and sat upright, unleashing his golden stare on her grandfather. "What kind of place do you run? Had she been home with me, James wouldn't have stepped one foot on the property without my knowing."

Rage flickered in Gavin's eyes. "I run a peaceful

pack!" he barked. "And I don't take kindly to others interfering."

"I don't give two shits what you take kindly to! Your granddaughter is out there, in the hands of some fucking psychopath, all because your people don't have a lick of sense about security! For fuck's sake, your grandson is dying in the next room! You might be dominant, but you are *not* an alpha."

Gavin blinked and stepped back, his hands stained with Wyatt's blood.

Wyatt turned with a feral snarl and locked his stare on Amberly. "Get these fucking bullets out of me!"

"You think that's going to be enough?" Gavin grunted. "The silver is poisoning you!"

"I'm done wasting time here. Patch me up so I can get the fuck out of here and find Sky."

Amberly flicked a startled glance to Gavin and waited for his nod. Once she had it, she got to work. He knew the risks, knew what the damned silver bullets were capable of. But none of that mattered.

The moment Sky's sister-in-law finished plucking out the last bullet, he shot off the table. Pain lanced through his chest and he staggered forward, his hand barely catching him against the wall.

"You aren't strong enough to get her back," Gavin said behind him.

Wyatt's response was a low snarl. "Thank you, Captain Obvious. But you're fucked in the head if you think I'm going to sit back and hope this resolves itself."

A strong hand came down on his shoulder. "Let me

help you. I know the land. We can track Sky's scent together."

With a heavy breath, Wyatt glanced up at Gavin. The silver had already begun to spread through his system. He felt the toxin in his blood, slowing his reflexes. Even his wolf was silent, hidden in the darkest recess of his mind. He needed time to heal, not that he had any. It rankled him to accept the offer, but he had no choice. Sky was in danger, and he'd be damned if his pride cost him her life.

———

Sky's eyes opened to darkness.

Within ten seconds, she went from dead asleep to alert and panicked. The last things she remembered were Noah, practically gutted by a gleaming knife, and then a sharp prick against the side of her neck. She sucked in a deep breath—

A clammy hand clapped over her mouth. Next to her, a monster rose, a pair of amber eyes burning in the darkness. "Don't scream, Skylar."

She shivered at the sound of his voice, a whimpered protest slipping through his fingers as she struggled against the bonds that held her to the bed.

"It's just me," he whispered, as though that would alleviate her fears.

*It's just me*...a statement reserved for a friend. James Griffon was *not* her friend. The few times they'd spoken, he'd peppered her with insensitive questions about her mother and her job. He'd *never* alluded to any sort of attraction to her. Not that it would have mattered.

Her wide eyes flicked to his, and she mumbled a question against his palm.

He shook his head. "I can't understand you, sweetheart. If I remove my hand, do you promise not to scream?"

*No!* But she nodded emphatically, desperate to be rid of his touch.

His hand loosened, fingertips tracing the curve of her bottom lip. Rapture smoothed his face, his eyes dimming to the dark brown she was accustomed to. He'd fooled them all into believing he was human, suppressed his wolf until even his scent had changed.

She dampened her mouth. "Where am I?"

"Home," he whispered, his fingers trailing down the curve of her neck. She drew in a shuddered breath, the faded aroma of her mother's possessions tickling her nose. *The cabin.* Horror quickened her pulse—he'd been the one maintaining it. "So beautiful. I've never had the chance to tell you that." He gazed up at her, a perverse grin warping his mouth. "But now I can, every day for the rest of our lives."

*Oh, God.* The last person she wanted to spend forever with was him. The only one she wanted was Wyatt.

*Wyatt.* She forced herself to swallow. Was he alive? Everything had happened so fast. The sharp crack of the gun and the sight of him crumpling to the ground... *Oh, God, Wyatt!* Werewolves could survive a great deal, but

James wouldn't bring a regular gun. A shot to the heart with a silver bullet was enough to kill any werewolf.

James' touch dragged her thoughts back to the grim present. His fingers trailed across her chest as he traced the curve of her naked body with singular purpose. She couldn't restrain her shudder. He paused, a shadow darkening his face. Her stomach twisted when she gazed down her length. He'd taken her clothes, stripped her nude. With her eyes squeezed shut, she dropped her head back against the pillow and willed away the tears that threatened to spill.

"I—I'm already mated," she whispered. "To Wyatt."

James bit out a harsh curse as the hand near her head tightened into a fist. "That doesn't matter," he assured himself. "Wyatt's dead."

*No.* She refused to believe that. She leaned as far away from him as possible and tugged on the restraints, gasping when silver bit into her flesh.

He glanced her way, his furious countenance softening when he found her straining away from him. "Sweetheart, don't. You'll hurt yourself."

Her teeth set into her lip as she jerked harder. Screw the silver. She needed *out.* She needed to find Wyatt. She needed free of this asshole.

Wyatt had to be alive. It was the only outcome she would accept. Alphas were tough bastards, and Wyatt was nothing if not an alpha. If anyone could brush off a silver bullet, it was him. And then he'd hunt down James, a thought that tugged the corner of her mouth.

"Sky!" James leaned over her and gripped her arms, pushing them down into the bed. "Lie still!"

*Screw that.* Instead, she opened her mouth and released a piercing scream. A sharp backhand lit up her cheek. Her head snapped into the pillow, tears pricking her eyes—eyes she desperately wanted to keep. She had to do whatever it took to keep him from snapping.

James hadn't taken her far. Her mother's cabin was located on the edge of pack land, some eight miles from her grandfather's estate.

Wyatt would come, but she'd have to help him find her.

## 19

In all his years as an alpha, Wyatt had never felt such terror. He'd never allowed himself to feel anything beyond friendship or lust for anyone. The females he took to his bed had inspired excitement, but nothing as emotionally crippling as love. He'd told her that she robbed him of his control, but it was deeper than that. He worried for her, feared that he'd lose her just as he'd found her.

*No.* He shook his head. He couldn't think like that. He needed to get his shit together. He was the fucking alpha, for crying out loud. That meant calm and clear-headed in a crisis.

Together, Gavin and Wyatt stared down the multiple treads cut out of the land. Half an hour ago, they'd discovered that one of Gavin's all-terrain vehicles was missing. With a growl, Wyatt relinquished his death grip on the handlebars of his quad and rubbed his temples. There were far too many tracks, the majority from

Gavin's people. Thankfully, they had their noses to follow.

"How the hell did you not hear an ATV in the distance?"

Gavin sighed and threw up his hands. "In case you hadn't noticed, at the time there was a lot of chaos and shouting. It isn't every day that my territory is breached by a psychopathic killer."

Revving the engine, Wyatt burst forward, his nose leading the way up over a steep hill. "What's in this direction?"

"About four miles south is the freeway," Gavin shouted back. "If they've reached it—"

"They could be anywhere," Wyatt snarled.

Ripping over the terrain, Wyatt reached deep into his psyche to rouse his wolf. He needed the mate connection, but the friggin' silver was blocking it. Worse, the vibrations were jarring his body. Every bump in the path sent a scorching ribbon of pain through his torso. At this rate, he would bleed out before they found her.

*Don't focus on the physical pain.* It meant nothing in comparison to losing Sky, and *that* was a future he refused to consider. It didn't matter that his temperature had spiked, or that his strength was failing, or that his shirt dripped with blood. The silver would work its way out of his system, or it wouldn't. He had no control over that.

*Fucking silver.*

At the freeway, he slammed on the breaks. "Her smell is fainter here."

Gavin pulled up next to him. "They could have gotten into a vehicle."

Or the amount of traffic had diluted her trail. *Shit*, James could have had a vehicle waiting on the side of the road. He sagged against the front of the quad, his breath labored. Thankfully, Gavin chose not to comment on his state of declining health.

"What's across the freeway?" he mumbled.

Gavin shook his head. "The ocean is less than twenty miles away—" His breath hitched and he swung a wide glance toward Wyatt.

"What?"

"Ivy's cabin."

"Who?"

"My daughter!"

*The cabin.* Wyatt peered across the road. He saw nothing over the rolling hills, not that he expected to. "How far?"

"Maybe four miles?"

"Go," Wyatt growled. Easing on the gas, he zipped across the street. Half a mile later, Sky's scent blossomed. The cabin it was.

"Can you handle this?" Gavin demanded behind him.

It only took one well-placed hit to kill someone; his years of underground fighting had taught him that. Wyatt leapt from the quad and shifted. Pain seared his chest and gut, and he staggered a step forward. He drew in a labored breath and then shook himself out.

"I'll take that as a yes," Gavin muttered before gunning forward with Wyatt hot on his heels.

Even if it killed him, he'd finish this tonight.

---

"Don't touch me!" Blind with panic, Sky scrambled on the bed as best she could with her limbs restrained. "Wyatt!"

"Stop it!" A sharp crack sent her head reeling once more. "I don't understand! What is happening?" His muttered words echoed in her ears. "It isn't supposed to be this way. You're supposed to *love me!*"

With a deep breath, Sky wrenched on the bonds with all her strength, manic laughter spilling from her lips when they gave the slightest bit. A little bit more and maybe she could free her one wrist.

"I love you!" James shouted before he stooped over her.

His throaty growl skated across her cheek, and before she could wrench away, his dry mouth crashed against hers, his slimy tongue penetrating the seam of her lips. Sky squeezed her eyes shut and gave a muffled protest as she tugged on the loosened bond. Fingers groped at her, grabbing and twisting her into submission. *No!* She refused to let this happen.

She gave a desperate cry and jerked her head to the side, chest heaving. "I don't love you."

He jolted back from her, eyes blazing. The moment James staggered away from her, she knew. She'd pushed him beyond his limits. He grasped the sides of his head and swung around, his mumbled words echoing his delusional endearment over and over.

His shadow loomed over her, rage alight in his eyes. Sky fell still, the cold hand of fear gripping her heart. "You're just like the rest of them," he spat, hate twisting his face into a grotesque mask. "An eager slut ready to please the first man that will have you. You tease and taunt, bat your beautiful eyes at any man that glances your way, and then drop him where he stands. But I can fix that." His chest heaved. "You think any man will want you after I ruin you?"

Her breath quickened.

"No man wants damaged goods." Clawed fingers started for her eyes.

Sky released a bloodcurdling shriek, tears dampening her face as she squirmed against him. She had to delay him, had to break through the insanity that held him captive. "James, James...wait. Wait, please wait."

"I've waited long enough! For three years I've waited! But did you ever give me the time of day? And now—now you're going to suffer like I did. You don't want me? *Fine.*"

Pressure pushed into her cheeks, his claws slipping beneath her flesh as he started for her eyes. Sky cried out and writhed against the bed, her hips bucking. Pain scalded her skin, ripping another whimper from her cracked lips. *This can't be happening!*

A sudden crash shook the cabin walls. Cursing, James' hands vanished from her face. Sky moaned and sank into the mattress, her cheeks soaked with tears and blood.

"Skylar!"

She knew that voice! "Grandpa!" she wailed, once

again pulling with all her strength. Her teeth latched onto her bottom lip as she struggled, determined to get free. "Get me out of here!"

A savage howl tore through the cabin. Sky gasped, her struggle forgotten in the wake of that beautiful sound. *Wyatt*! He wasn't dead! Her heart soared with hope.

"Not possible!" James whirled around, his gaze wide and unblinking as he stared down at Skylar. "You can't have her! She's mine!"

With a snarl, he lunged for her, claws extended. Skylar closed her eyes and screamed. She never felt the graze of James' claws. Air ruffled by her head as Wyatt slammed into James, their force carrying them right through the wall. A chorus of brutal shouts and snarls echoed through the cabin.

"Skylar..."

"Grandpa!" She twisted against the bed, fresh tears washing down her face. "Get me out of these!"

Gavin rushed to her side and grasped the thick chains. "I got you, baby girl." Grunting, he strained his muscles and pulled with all his strength until finally the first one snapped. Together, they wrenched on the remaining bonds. Once freed, she slid off the bed and coerced her wolf forward. Wyatt was injured; she'd scented his blood the moment he'd burst into the room. There was no way in hell she would abandon him.

Once in wolf form, she bolted toward the gaping hole in the wall.

Her grandfather's large frame dove in front of her. "What are you doing? Get out of here!"

She gnashed her teeth next to his leg before ducking

around him and racing toward Wyatt. Her breath caught at the astounding sight that greeted her. James' meaty arm was locked around Wyatt's throat, fingers digging into his wounds. Scrambling against the floor, Wyatt couldn't find purchase, and the sound of his strangled breath terrified her.

Gathering her strength, Sky rushed forward, intent on pouncing, when her grandfather swept her out of the way. She careened across the floor on her side, her head crashing into the wall, but through her blurred vision, she watched as Gavin drove his fist into James' mouth. Freed from his hold, Wyatt danced backward and shook his head. His racking cough encouraged her, but the small puddles of blood dotting the floor didn't.

A desperate tone entered the fight. James swung wildly, his golden eyes burning with conviction. He had to know he wouldn't survive this fight, but he seemed dedicated to taking them down with him.

Sky picked herself up. It was now or never. Wyatt was stumbling on his feet, and her grandfather was no match for James. About to leap into the fray, a panicked bark fell from her mouth when James' claws slashed through her grandfather's chest and belly.

*No!*

She leapt, claws and teeth extended. She poured every ounce of hate into her attack, every bit of fear he'd bred into her for the past year.

Eyes narrowed, she slammed into his chest and spilled them to the ground.

*Don't hesitate.*

She lunged with a dark snarl, her teeth sealing

around his throat. His fists hammered at her, but Skylar held on. Allowing her wolf to take control, she clamped her jaws and tore out James' throat.

Silence befell the cabin.

Panting for air, Sky stumbled away from his lifeless body and staggered to the nearest corner, where she emptied her stomach. Her body and soul ached, but she couldn't think about that now. She pushed to her feet and limped toward her grandfather's mangled body, head hung low. With a sharp whine, she lowered onto her belly and inched closer, but the wretched scent of lacerated bowels confirmed his death.

She tipped her head back and released a mournful howl. The harrowing sound poured from her lips, until all that remained was grief. Soon, Wyatt joined in, his resonate howl tuned to hers. To her wolf ears, it was a beautiful sound, one worthy of her grandfather.

Emotionally spent, Sky took her next cue from Wyatt, and together they shifted back. The second she stood on two legs, he swept her into his arms and crushed her against him.

"You're hurt," she whispered.

"I don't care." His injured chest rumbled against her. "Give me this."

"Wyatt—"

"Sky. Don't argue with me right now. I need this."

She sank into his embrace, her eyes slipping closed. She needed it as much as he did, but the fear of him bleeding out made her anxious.

"Don't do this to me again, all right?"

"What, get kidnapped by a bloody psychopath?"

"Yes, that."

She nodded. It definitely wasn't on her top ten list. "Grandpa..."

His arms tightened for a brief second before he finally released her. "I know. We'll get someone out here immediately to tend to him."

"Why did he dive in like that? He could have hung back, could have let us fight James."

"No, he couldn't," Wyatt murmured. "He loved you, Sky. A great deal. And alphas protect those they love."

She jerked her chin up. "What?"

"I was in his office. There are pictures of you everywhere. He might not have liked how rebellious you were, but he loved you."

Sky's bottom lip trembled. "He never told me. He was always so angry around me."

Sighing, Wyatt pulled her into his chest once more. Tears slipped down her cheeks, her control fractured. She wanted nothing more than to sob away the grief, but she had to take care of her grandfather. She owed him that. Wiping her eyes with her palms, she gasped when she touched the gashes in her cheeks, a hair's breadth from her eyes. Still, she was lucky. Barbara, Erica, Jody Anne...even Trinity.

"Wyatt?"

He dropped his chin and met her gaze, his irises rimmed in gold.

"Take me home."

He nodded, brushed a light kiss against her brow, then led her away from her mother's cabin. It could burn, for all she cared.

# EPILOGUE

Skylar brushed her hands down her borrowed skirt and blouse and stole a quick glimpse into Wyatt's recovery room. "How is he?"

"Irritable," Amberly said with a wry smile. "I don't think I've ever had such a wretched patient before. Are you sure he'll be a good mate?"

"Yes," Sky murmured. "Without a doubt."

"It *was* pretty impressive how he shot out of here to find you, even riddled with silver as he was."

Sky ducked her head and hid the blush that chased across her cheeks. Sawyer had gone to great lengths to tell her exactly how rude her mate had been. Amberly had simply chuckled and patted her brother on his head.

"How was Gavin's funeral?"

Tears sprang to her eyes, but Sky nodded. "As to be expected. No funeral is ever easy."

Her sister-in-law released a slow breath and wrapped her arms around Sky. "No, I suppose not."

"I'm sorry you couldn't attend."

Amberly nodded and rested her head in the crook of Sky's shoulder. "Someone had to stay and make sure your man stayed in bed. I swear, the moment you left the house, I had to threaten to sedate him."

"He's worried."

"Tell him to stop," Amberly murmured. "The bad guy has been defeated. The day is saved."

Skylar chuckled.

"You two can stop talking about me like I'm not here."

The two women dissolved into giggles at the sound of Wyatt's dejected voice. Poor man had been bedridden for two days while his system worked out the silver. It had made him one unhappy alpha.

"When can he leave?" Sky asked once she caught her breath.

"Ah, he's good to go. Take it easy. No more chasing villains through the hills, and don't forget to visit with Noah before you leave."

Brushing her lips across Amberly's cheek, Sky stepped into the room and met Wyatt's stern gaze. "Feeling better?" she asked as she crossed toward him.

His jaw muscle leaped. "How's Noah?"

She would have laughed, if not for his serious tone. For two days, he'd been inquiring after Noah, requesting updates every hour. It'd been touch-and-go for a while, but Amberly had finally deemed him stable.

"He's going to be fine. The blade missed his heart, but it was silver. He had some troubles purging it from his system."

Relief loosened his jaw. "Good. Come here."

With a sheepish grin, Sky took his hand and allowed him to pull her onto the bed with him. As horrible as the past two days had been, Wyatt had been her one shining star. Her family's pack had much to deal with. The loss of an alpha was never easy, and the power struggle had already begun. Not to mention one of their youngest males was bedridden, his life almost lost to trouble that she had brought with her. It had made for some awkward dinners.

"You need to stop looking at me like that," Sky murmured before brushing a kiss against his lips.

"Like what?" He blinked puppy-dog eyes at her.

"Like you're going to lose me. James is dead, and we're alive. You can't be with me every minute of the day, you know."

"I can try."

She shook her head. "Then don't blame me when I kick you in the nuts again."

Wyatt laughed and then groaned. "Don't make me laugh."

"Still hurts?" The silver bullets had shredded his insides. It was a miracle he'd survived.

"Nah."

Which meant *yes*. Big, bad alpha, afraid to admit how much pain he was in.

"When do you want to leave?" Sky asked.

"Tomorrow morning. Bale called while you were at Gavin's funeral. The hospital is releasing Trinity in three days. I'd like to be there for her."

"So would I." It broke her heart knowing that she had

brought such tragedy into Trinity's life. The woman had only wanted to be her friend, and now her life would never be the same. The bastard had torn out her eyes and left her for dead. If she could kill James again, she would.

"He and Harley have been looking into James' past. Seems the Appalachian Pack had exiled him about four years ago. He was more concerned with making a name for himself than he was involved with his pack. If his house was any indication, he'd locked onto you almost immediately afterward."

Sky shivered. She didn't want to think about James ever again. Her life was finally her own again, and she intended on spending it with her very prickly alpha.

The same prickly alpha who was studying her with a serious air.

"What's wrong?"

"Absolutely nothing," he assured her. "Reassuring myself that you're still here with me."

She lifted his hand to her mouth and brushed her lips against the tips of his fingers. Had he arrived a few moments later, who knew the condition he would have found her in. Her recent nightmares had given her many scenarios to ponder. In the dark of night, she still felt James' rank breath against her skin, felt his claws slicing at her eyes.

Clearing her throat, she guided her thoughts down a more pleasant avenue. "I'm not going anywhere."

Relief softened his face.

"Have I thanked you, yet?" she asked. "You know, for risking your own life to save mine?"

"You'll never have to. I couldn't let him..." He

brushed his fingers down her cheek, drawing a purr from deep within her throat. Since *that* night, he hadn't gone longer than an hour without touching her. And she hadn't objected. She wanted James' touch stricken from her body. Unfortunately, the cuts on either side of her eyes would leave permanent scars. "I'm grateful I found you in time."

Sky smiled and wound their fingers together. "Thank you. I wish we could have saved my grandfather."

A dark emotion crossed Wyatt's face. "He loved you. You know that, now. It's too bad you hadn't heard it from him."

She shrugged, her mouth turning down.

"Skylar, I love you."

She blinked. They were mates, but neither had uttered those three little words yet. Honestly, she'd never expected to hear them from Wyatt—she'd known from the start that he wasn't one to broadcast his emotions. He kept everything so close to his chest, protected by his tough exterior.

"I never want you to go through life wondering if I do. And I never want to be taken from you without you knowing—"

"Wyatt."

"—let me finish. I've never told anyone I loved them before. But I love *you*. And when we get home, I want you with me forever, as my mate and my wife."

Sky's head spun. Just when she thought she knew him, he changed the game. She met his steeled gaze, her mouth suddenly dry. "I love you too," she finally whispered, her voice thick with emotion.

"Yeah?"

She nodded, blinking back the silly tears that had sprung to her eyes.

"Good." He gave a nervous laugh. "That's really good. It won't be easy. I know that. You hate having an alpha and reject all form of dominance, but I think—"

"We'll make it work," she said, her voice stronger. "There's bound to be a little clashing between two dominant wolves, but we can make it work."

He chuckled under his breath. "I have to admit, I was expecting a little resistance. Maybe a little hair pulling, some biting..."

With a playful smile, she leaned forward and said in a husky voice, "Happy to oblige."

She laid her parted mouth against his neck and gave a little nip as her fingers slid through his hair. Wyatt growled against her, his grip tightening on her ass and wrenching her flush against him.

"Sky..."

"Wyatt," she teased. Her tongue flicked out and licked his neck as she made her way to his ear.

"*Christ*, Sky. You're playing with fire, here."

"Mm, the doctor cleared you, so, light me up."

His grip turned to steel, and with a savage growl, he brought her mouth down on his. Sky sank into him, her arms slipping around his neck as she awaited the ride of her life.

This was how it would always be with Wyatt, and she wouldn't have had it any other way. He might be the dangerous alpha who always got his way, but she'd claimed him, and that was all that mattered.

# ABOUT THE AUTHOR

Gwen Knight is a Canadian girl currently living in Jasper, AB. She graduated from the University of Lethbridge with a degree in Archaeology and Geography. Her interests consist of playing in the dirt, designing elaborate snow forts, boating, and archery. You can also subscribe to her newsletter here.

*For more information:*
www.gwenknight.ca

## WHISPERS IN THE DARK SNEAK PEAK

She didn't want to die.

Danica strained for breath as she scrambled through the surrounding trees. Usually, the forest served as her second home, but tonight, the land was treacherous. She slipped on the ice, and the sleet tore at her face as she struggled against an ongoing blizzard.

Over the fierce wind, she caught the faint echo of laughter as her attackers took chase. Bloodthirsty bastards. Every move she made, the blinding light from their trucks found her. All part of the hunt. They *wanted* her to shift. She could hear it in their jeers, taunting the beast within her.

"You can't run forever!"

Danica whimpered and banked a hard right, her clawed fingers digging into the nearest tree. Her wolf bayed in her head, pleading with her to stop and change. These men didn't stand a chance against a wolf, but by the time she shifted, they'd have her. And screaming for help was pointless. The assholes had chased her up into the mountains. No one would hear her up here.

Still, when a bullet slammed into the tree to the left of her head, she let loose a bloodcurdling shriek. Her wolf was so desperate to take over. Four legs were faster than two, and her fangs could rip out a throat faster than they could shoot. She couldn't risk it, though. Couldn't waste the precious time. Her only option was to escape.

But even that seemed hopeless.

She skidded to a stop and shot a frantic glance up the nearest pine. Was it tall enough? They had no hounds on her trail. Could she climb it quickly enough and escape them? Her fingers were numb and her legs stiff. But she couldn't run forever.

Cursing under her breath, she darted toward the base of the tree. Thick claws sprung from her fingers and burrowed into the bark. She shifted her weight, about to climb, when...*snap.*

An agonizing cry tore from her throat, the sound deafening even above the wind. Searing pain pierced her calf and brought her to her knees. Tears streaming down her cheeks, she glanced at her leg, her eyes widening at the sight of her sizzling blood. Trenched in her flesh and muscle was something metal...something *silver.* A bear trap.

With a sob, she grasped the snare, then gave another cry when it burned her fingers.

A frantic glance around revealed dozens of these traps, all laid out by the trees. Danica's head whipped around, and she watched as the lights grew closer. The bastards had planned this all along. They'd chased her up into the mountains where they'd laid traps.

Seized by raw panic, she bit down on her lip and wedged her fingers between the sharp teeth. Inch by inch, she pried it open. *Just a little more...*

A branch snapped, and the ground shifted beneath her. Before she could move, something heaved her into the air by her injured leg. Danica screamed, her eyes squeezing shut as she choked back the bile rising in her throat.

She couldn't give up. Their trucks were too close for her liking, their lights flickering in the darkness as they bore down on her. Whimpering, she sucked in a deep breath and reached for the trap. Her fingers barely brushed the metal. From this angle, prying herself free was impossible.

The loudest truck rumbled to a stop in front of her, the lights blinding her. *Oh, God.* She'd tried so hard to escape. Fresh tears slipped into her hair as she listened to a footed approach.

"Well, looky what we found."

Danica's watery gaze flicked toward the voice. His silhouette took shape within the faint light. She scoured his features in search of something familiar, only to realize he was a stranger with a face of shadows.

"Looks like we caught ourselves a nice treat, boys."

His men jeered as they fanned out behind him. One by one, their presences blocked the light until finally, she could see them and more importantly, their weapons. Who the hell were these men? And what did they want with her?

"Awful late for a young thing like you to be out and about, wouldn't you say?"

Danica reached for her leg again, a sob slipping past her lips when she fell back upside down. "Please. I—I don't know what you want from me. I just want to go home..."

"I'm afraid that's not an option." The leader shook his head, his jaw tight as he studied her length.

Her tears dripped into the snow.

"So, what exactly are you doing out so late at night?" he demanded.

She released a tremulous breath. She and a couple of pack mates had decided to go for a run tonight. Their first in a while, thanks to their alpha's decree that they stay out of the woods. A run that had led them up into the mountains, but they'd separated after chasing around a few deer. Werewolves weren't a secret—hadn't been in over ten years —so they hadn't kept their presence a secret. But that hardly meant she would admit it aloud to hunters armed with guns and silver traps. Clearly, they weren't up here hunting elk.

"You were running with...what do you call it? Your pack?"

Her eyes widened, and she shook her head.

Rage narrowed his gaze. "Don't *lie* to me. You think I can't see those claws of yours? You're one of *them*."

Danica inwardly crumpled, and a whimper slipped past her lips. "We were running. That's all," she whispered as her gaze skimmed each of their faces, committing them to memory. None of them possessed an ounce of sympathy, and the scent of their rage and hatred poisoned the air. "Please, I'm not what you think. Let me go."

"Is that so?" The leader strode forward, his rifle in hand.

Moonlight slipped through the trees, illuminating him in an ambient glow that might have made him handsome were it not for the madness within.

"Seems to me you're *exactly* what I think you are. You know, we've been hunting for one of you beasts for over a month now." He spat on the ground, his face twisted with fury.

"No," she whimpered. "I'm not a beast. I swear. I'm not. I swear. Please—"

The butt of his rifle slammed into her gut.

Danica snarled. Fangs sprouted in her mouth, and her claws lengthened, but the gun aimed at her face convinced her to rein it in.

"Not a beast, hey? Sure looks to me like there's something nasty in you. What, you think we're just gonna sit back and let you monsters slaughter us? Think we're gonna sit back and take it?"

Danica's gums ached as her fangs retracted. Her wolf howled in her head, desperate to rip into these men until nothing remained but bone meal.

"You abominations took my daughter from me!" His voice shivered with rage. "Raped her, sliced her up like she was nothing more than a meal!"

The air vanished from Danica's lungs. *Oh, God.* That was what this was about. The murders. Her alpha had warned them about possible backlash from the community after a psychotic werewolf had killed three human women.

"No...no." She shook her head. "That wasn't us. That wolf wasn't even part of our pack!"

"Shut up!" The next blow took her across the jaw, stunning her into silence. "There was barely anything left for us to bury! Did you like it? Did you all take a turn before cutting out her eyes?" he shouted in agony and slammed his rifle into her cheek.

Danica cried out, blood warm on her tongue. "James Griffon was a psycho! My alpha *killed* him!"

"Alpha..." He sneered and stepped back from her, scoping his audience with a feral gleam in his eyes. "Hear that? *Alpha*. Like a real fucking pack of wolves. More animal than human, aren't you?"

"No..."

"Don't worry. We know how to take care of monsters like you."

"Please—"

Crazed laughter silenced her. "*Please*, she says. You know, I'll bet my daughter begged too. *Begged* him not to touch her. But he didn't listen, and neither will I. We're going to teach all you so-called shifters what it means to mess with humans. You might be bigger and stronger, but there are more of us." A cold glint shimmered in his eyes as he turned toward his own pack. "Gary. What's a werewolf pelt fetch these days?"

Fear cramped Danica's stomach.

A figure unfolded from a nearby tree, the only spot of light that of the burning cigarette dangling from his lips.

"Ten grand...give or take," he muttered around the filter. "Another two for the fangs."

Danica thrashed against the trap, then screamed when the metal teeth cut deeper.

"Ten grand is a nice number." The leader turned back to her, his lips lifted in a cruel grin. "Ain't no natural wolf ever fetch me that price before. So, we're going to need to you to shift, or whatever you call it. Rumor has it pain can trigger the change."

She shook her head, her eyes widening when the group closed in on her. "You think we're the monsters? Take a look around! You're talking about skinning an innocent girl!"

His laughter chilled her blood. "Nothing innocent about you. The devil's dog is what you are. Just because you know how to walk on two legs don't make you anything more than that." Holding her gaze, he reached for his side and brandished a long, curved blade.

"You're fucking insane!" Danica struggled against the trap's hold, praying that it snapped through her shin bone. Anything to give her a sporting chance.

The leader grabbed her by the earlobe, then flicked his wrist. Unadulterated pain cut through the side of her head, and a sharp scream rang through the trees, but it wasn't until she paused for breath that she realized the sound had come from her.

"Yell all you like, sweetheart." The bloodied blade caught the moonlight as he stepped back, flaunting her severed ear in his hand. "Ain't no one coming for you tonight."

No one did.

**ALSO BY GWEN KNIGHT**

*Wolffe Peak Series*
Whispers in the Dark

*Harlequin Cravings*
Her Alpha Protector
A Hunter's Passion

*Amelia Winters Series*
Marked

*Souls of Salem Chronicles*
A Touch of Soul

*Cursed Holiday Series*
Death by Mistletoe
Death by Chocolate

*Isa Fae Collection*

Reaper

Made in the USA
Columbia, SC
01 March 2018